THE OAKS
PREPARATORY
SCHOOL

Shetland Summer

by Billie Touchstone Signer
illustrations by Bob Bliss

St. Paul Books & Media

Library of Congress Cataloging-in-Publication Data

Signer, Billie Touchstone, 1930-
    Shetland summer / written by Billie Touchstone Signer ;
  illustrated by Bob Bliss.
        p.   cm.
    ISBN 0-8198-6884-1 (pbk. : alk. paper)
    [1. Ponies—Fiction. 2. Ozark Mountains—Fiction.] I. Bliss, Bob, ill.
II. Title.
PZ7. S578Sh   1990
[fic]—dc19   88-18480
                                                                      CIP
                                                                       AC

Printed and published in the U.S.A. by St. Paul Books and Media
50 St. Paul's Avenue, Boston, MA 02130

St. Paul Books and Media is the publishing house of the Daughters of St. Paul,
an international congregation of women religious serving the Church with the
communications media.

    1   2   3   4   5   6   7   8   9   95   94   93   92   91   90

To Mary,
who lights up my life...

Contents

CHAPTER ONE

Getting Acquainted

Mag jerked at the tangles in her long, blond hair. She had to hurry if she wanted to ride the new Shetland pony. She eased the comb through once more, gliding over the snarls hidden underneath.

"There, that should do," she said aloud. She put the comb on the dresser and called from her bedroom: "Mother, I finished combing my hair. I'm going to ride Glory now."

"Don't be long. The hired men are here to work in the hayfield, and I'll need your help with their lunch."

"All right." Mag took the bridle off the door hook and sighed. "She probably won't let me ride her, but I'm going to try again."

Her mother smiled. "Be careful, dear. That pony is as high-spirited as you are."

Mag shrugged her shoulders. "I know," she replied, and bounced onto the shady porch of the big farmhouse where she had lived all her life. From the porch she could see the meadow and the haying crew. The men, dark-skinned and muscular, came every year in a big rattling truck from somewhere beyond the mountains.

Haying season didn't only mean work for the men in the fields: Mrs. Henderson prepared mountains of food on the big wood-burning stove, and it was Mag's job to keep the wood box filled with fuel. During meals, Mag made sure that the workers' glasses were filled with tea and the platters were refilled with the golden cornbread and hot biscuits which disappeared almost as soon as her mother pulled them from the oven. Usually Mag had to make trip after trip to the back porch, too. There, inside a wash tub, a huge block of ice was wrapped in a clean quilt. Ice was a novelty; the Hendersons bought it only during haying season or on special occasions. As the girl chopped at the ice with a sharp pick, she would slip a sliver or two into her mouth to enjoy the delicious coolness.

For now, though, she had some time to herself. Bridle in hand, she headed for the fields. Lady, an old collie, looked up as Mag skipped off the porch, but was too comfortable to follow the girl.

The rocks were hot along the trail, and Mag's bare feet moved over them quickly. "Glad we don't have to pick peas today," she said aloud. She was tired of peas, peas, and more peas. They had to be picked every other day during the summer. She knew her mother must be tired, too.

Mag stopped for a second. Honeysuckle vines, thick and sweet-smelling, hid the pasture fence on one end. Three hummingbirds with long, slender bills were helping themselves to nectar from the blossoms. Their wings were vibrating so fast, the birds were "humming" in flight. They seemed to stop in mid-air before plunging head first into the sweet liquid. Mag liked to watch them while they fluttered about.

The girl again hurried toward the gate, scanning the pasture for the pony her father was boarding for a city friend. He had wanted to sell Glory to the Hendersons, but Mag's father, for some reason, did not like ponies.

From the far corner of the pasture, the honey-colored filly glared at Mag. Glory had a long mane and tail, and a coat that Mrs. Henderson declared was the same color as Mag's hair.

Mag held the bridle behind her back, out of sight. "Well, my new-found friend, why are you looking at me like that? You ought to be more than satisfied. You've thrown me off every single time I've gotten on your back. And you might today, but we're going around again." Glory, of course, had other ideas. She sounded a whinny and raced across the small pasture to the other side near the fence.

Mag ran after her. "You're not going to get the best of me, you ornery little thing!" The girl's long legs carried her swiftly across the pasture.

Glory had not been trained and didn't know the meaning of obedience, but Mag was determined to teach her before the end of the summer, when the Roarks would come for her. They would probably take Glory to the auction, unless Mag could convince her father to keep her. That would take a miracle.

Mag slowed down as she neared the pony. "Oh, well, I have most of the summer with you. A lot can happen in a summer." The pony eyed the long-legged creature as she inched closer.

"There's one thing, though, young lady. At least when you throw me off, I don't have far to fall."

Glory nodded her head as though agreeing with Mag.

Mag laughed aloud as she put her hand on the skittish pony. She let the bridle slide slowly to the ground, and with her other hand eased a lump of sugar from her pocket.

"I was going to give you this yesterday, but you acted so bad, I didn't think you deserved it."

Glory smelled the sugar and then ate it quickly. Mag reached down behind her and picked up the bridle. She slipped it over the pony's head and eased the bit between the pony's teeth.

"I sure didn't think you'd let me do that without a fight," the girl remarked, surprised. "You're very unpredictable. That's what my mother says about me." She sighed. "People just never know what you're going to do next."

She kept talking softly as she crawled onto the pony's back. She could feel her heart beating in her throat. "Please don't be afraid of me, Glory; you're so pretty and I love you already."

Mag steadied herself for the usual bucking spree, but to her surprise, Glory stood perfectly still.

The pony's first instinct was to toss Mag off her back, but the little blond girl with sugar in the pockets of her faded jeans wasn't so frightening to the Shetland today.

"If I can convince Daddy to let me keep you, I'll save all my money for a little saddle." Mag stroked the pony's neck. "I'll bet you'd like that."

Glory walked slowly along, very conscious of the load on her back. She stopped often, nibbling at the grass.

"Now, Glory, don't do that when I'm riding you. You can eat later." Mag jerked gently at the reins.

The pony's instinct won. Glory lowered her head to buck, but Mag quickly slid off her back. The race was on! The pony ran her fastest, the bridle reins flying in the breeze.

Mag ran after her, yelling with every breath, her face as red as a rooster's comb.

Across the patch went the Shetland-Welsh pony with Mag in hot and angry pursuit.

Suddenly, Glory stopped and began eating grass.

Mag walked up and took the reins. She put her free hand on her hip and said with determination: "Now, you listen to me.

I'm getting back on and riding you to the barn. I'm going to brush your coat while we talk. We've just got one summer, and I want to enjoy you."

With that, Mag climbed back on the pony.

Glory had definitely met her match.

CHAPTER TWO

Don't Cry, Glory

Mag brushed Glory until she was as sleek and shiny as a show pony. "You're so beautiful," she spoke to the pony. "And you know what? Daddy says you're half Welsh and that's why you're bigger than regular Shetlands." Mag stepped back to get a better look at Glory. "I read once that Shetlands originally came from a very cold place called the Shetland Islands, and that you're small because of the long, hard winters without much to eat." She worked again on Glory's mane. "And the other half of you, the Welsh part, well, that came from Wales, another cold place a long way from here. Your ancestors worked in the mines, pulling heavy wagons of coal all day long." Mag sighed. Glory nickered as if to say, "Is that so?"

"Aren't you glad you don't live in those old places?"

Mag put the brush aside and began to plait Glory's long golden mane. She looked around for something to hold it in place, then removed the blue hair clasp from her own hair and snapped it into place at the end of the mane. "Now, don't you look sassy?" she teased as she hugged the little pony.

Mag looked into Glory's face and saw tears. "What is it, girl? Why are you crying?" Mag looked everywhere on the pony to see if something was hurting her. "There it is, a big old burr."

Mag pulled it off. Then from the overhead shelf, she took down a jar of green salve and dabbed it on the sore. "Now, that ought to feel better soon." Glory whinnied her thanks.

The girl looked back into the pony's face. The tears had stopped. "It's most unusual, Glory, for a pony to cry. I'll have to tell Daddy about that." She put things back in place and led Glory out to the pasture, still thinking about the tears.

She looked up at the cloudless sky. The sun told her it was the middle of the morning—time to go and help her mother get lunch ready for the farm hands.

Glory ran swiftly across the pasture, and Mag laughed suddenly when she saw the blue hair clasp bobbing up and down as the pony ran.

———————

That evening after supper, Mag told her parents about Glory's tears.

Mr. Henderson knocked his pipe against the wood box before speaking. He was a man of few words. "No, Mag, horses don't cry—or at least they don't cry as people do. Sure, they can get something in their eyes and tears will come to wash it away, but crying because of a burr, no, I'm afraid that's not possible, honey."

"But, Daddy, if you could have seen her...." She leaned back in the porch swing. Why wouldn't he believe her?

"If I had seen her, Mag, I would still say she had something in her eyes, that's all." He filled his pipe carefully.

Mrs. Henderson pulled her rocker near her husband on the long, cool porch and sat down. "Well, honey, couldn't the animal be sensitive enough to shed tears? Who has proved they cannot?" A kind woman, Lenora Henderson had great compassion for animals.

Mag looked from one to the other.

Mr. Henderson lit his pipe before answering. Mag took a deep breath. She liked the smell of her father's pipe. "Lenora, common sense tells us animals don't have emotions like humans."

Mrs. Henderson pushed a strand of dark hair back into its bun on her neck. "Pain isn't an emotion as happiness and sadness are, Henry."

Mag knew her mother was right, but she felt uneasy when her parents called each other by their first names rather than the usual affectionate names.

Henry Henderson was tiring of the conversation and said firmly, "If you wish to believe such a fantasy, there's no harm in it, I suppose, but don't try to make me believe it."

"All right, Daddy. But I do agree with Mag: Glory was in pain."

Mag gave a big smile. How she loved her mother! "I wonder," Mag said to herself, "why it is that mothers always seem to understand?"

Mrs. Henderson looked at her daughter, who was deep in thought. "Where's your other clasp, Mag?"

Mag reached up to feel her hair, then put her hand over her mouth and giggled, "I put it in Glory's mane when I plaited it today."

Mrs. Henderson laughed aloud and then shook her head in bewilderment.

Mr. Henderson smiled, and then his face clouded. He stood up and started into the house. Suddenly he turned and faced Mag. "Remember, Magdalen, that Shetland leaves here in September."

She swallowed hard. Her father meant business when he called her that. "Yes, sir, I'll remember."

That night, Mag dreamed of Shetland-Welsh ponies all over the farm and even inside the house. She looked desperately for Glory, but they all looked alike. She ran about looking into each of their faces to see if they were crying. How else could she tell which one was Glory?

Mag woke up crying. Her tears had fallen on the freshly starched pillowcase. She wiped her eyes. How silly her dream had been.

Soon the sun began filtering through the white curtains. She jumped out of bed and knelt to say her prayers, something she did every day, or at least as often as she remembered. Before her "Amen," she could smell bacon and coffee.

Mag hastily got into her faded jeans and shirt, ran a brush through her hair to get the surface tangles out, then hurried to the kitchen.

The silly dream kept popping into her mind. She wondered if her daddy was right. "No," she thought to herself, "Glory did cry because of the burr. I just know it."

CHAPTER THREE

Pig Chase

The sun seemed hotter than usual as Mag plucked the peas to fill her pail. She adjusted the old straw hat her mother made her wear and looked at the cloudless sky. "Gosh," she sighed, "I must have picked a zillion peas in my life." Then she wondered if there was such a number as "zillion."

It really wasn't a big job; it was just monotonous. She could think of so many things she'd rather be doing.

In the next row, Mag's mother straightened up and wiped her brow with her apron. "Your pail full yet?"

"Just about." Mag stepped across the row to get a choice handful of almost black peas.

Mrs. Henderson smiled. "Tell you what. Why don't you and Glory go to the back of the farm and ride the fence row to see if you can find a hole. The piglets didn't come up this morning, and I'll just bet they're out."

"Goody. I'll be glad to do it." She hugged her mother and skipped happily from the field.

Her mother shook her head and smiled as she returned to her work.

―――――――――

"Slow down, Glory, so I can look for the hole the pigs came through." Glory slowed a bit, but seemed anxious to get back to her nice green pasture.

"Can't imagine why the silly things want out anyway. They have a mamma with lots of milk, a plot with plenty of green grass and cool water." Mag sighed, "Oh well, I guess pigs are like people, always looking for something they don't have."

Glory came to a halt and began nibbling at a tuft of grass growing between two rocks. "Glory, don't do that. You're going to have to learn that when you have a job to do, you do it first. Then you can do what you like afterwards." Glory didn't think so. Mag pulled on the reins.

"You know something? You and I are a lot alike." Glory nickered. "Well, we are. We have stubborn streaks a mile wide." Mag patted the pony's neck. "Guess that's why I love you so much."

Suddenly Mag shouted, "There's the hole. And there are the funny little pigs. They seem to play games all the time." She giggled as the young pigs spotted her and Glory. They ran squealing together in single file up the road alongside the fence. Inside the fence, the old sow, searching for tender grubs a short distance away, heard them and came running to their rescue. Glory and Mag were behind the piglets, which were now running beside the fence, and the sow was on the other side, trying to get to her babies.

"Just you wait a minute, old Mamma. Glory and I will herd them, and we'll all meet at the gate near the barn." The sow must not have understood Mag; she kept oinking and the pigs kept squealing. Glory was getting more nervous by the minute. After all, the Shetland had never herded cattle, much less a bunch of squealing pigs. The big sow, almost as tall as the pony, kept warning her not to come near the piglets. It was more than Glory could take.

She balked and just stood there, while Mag begged and nudged her in the side to try and get her going. Finally, the girl slid off Glory's back and pulled at the reins. She was upset. ''I hope Daddy does make you leave, Glory, if that's the way you're going to act when I need you. Come on, Glory, the pigs will go on past the gate, and we'll never get them back inside.'' Tears filled Mag's eyes as she pleaded. ''Please, Glory, Mother is depending on me to do this.''

Glory looked at Mag and gave a loud whinny.

Once more, Mag crawled onto Glory's back. This time Glory did just as she was told.

''You know, little pony, I just never know about you.'' Mag wiped her tears away with the back of her hand, and a smile broke through as they went off in the direction of the squealing pigs.

''Let's go, girl!'' Glory shot out and herded the pigs, keeping them near the fence in a straight line.

As they neared the gate, Mrs. Henderson was there to open it. She laughed aloud at the sight: Mag on the little pony, with her feet just a short distance from the ground, was herding the squealing baby pigs like so many head of cattle.

After the gate was shut, Mag, beaming all over, rode the pony up to her mother. ''Did you see that? Isn't she a fine cow pony—I mean, pig pony?'' She rubbed Glory's neck. Mrs. Henderson reached out and patted her, too.

''Yes, Mag, she is a fine little Shetland. But please, dear, don't become too attached to her. You know what your father said.'' Mrs. Henderson looked sad.

"I know, Mother, I know." But deep in her heart, Mag felt that something just had to happen to change her father's mind. How could she give Glory up now? How could she?

CHAPTER FOUR

The Old Mine Shaft

Mag finished her chores. Wasn't there anything exciting to do? An idea suddenly came to her!

"Mother, may I ride the pony over to the Fenton's house and get the honey?" Honey was an important part of sweetening for the Hendersons and most of their neighbors.

Mrs. Henderson was icing a cake. Without looking up, she responded, "Think you can manage the two jugs on Glory?"

"Sure, and it'll save you and Daddy a trip." Mag ran her finger over the rim of the bowl and licked the sweet icing. "Besides, I really like the Fentons."

Mrs. Henderson smiled. "Yes, and so do I." She put her arm around Mag and squeezed her. The girl was almost as tall as her mother. "I think you may go, but I want you to be especially careful. That road up Shiloh Mountain is narrow and very steep. If you hear a car, hug the bluff, not the edge of the road."

Mag squeezed her mother's hand. "I'll remember. Where are the jugs?"

Mrs. Henderson dried her hands on a bright dish towel and reached for two crocks with handles at the neck. "I'll get some heavy cord and run it through the handles so you can place them in front of you across the pony."

"That's a good idea. I'll get the quilt I use for a *saddle*."

Her mother tried to hide the smile that was tugging at the corners of her mouth. "Magdalen Henderson, your father said you weren't keeping the pony, so there's no need trying to work out a way to get a *saddle*."

They both burst into laughter.

Even in midsummer, Shiloh Mountain was beautiful. The winding, narrow road was heavily shaded all the way up. Wild flowers grew in abundance along the way. Red raspberries were beginning to ripen, and the bushes bowed gracefully under the weight of their fruit. Mag slid off Glory and ran to pick a handful. She plopped them all at once into her mouth. The sweet and sour juice ran deliciously down her throat. "Ummm! Glory, you like berries?"

She picked several and held them under Glory's nose. The pony turned her head away.

"No? Okay, then I'll eat 'em. I'll have to remember to tell Mother they're ready so we can pick some for jam." She wiped her sticky hands on her pants and climbed back onto the pony. "We're forever picking something," Mag sighed to herself.

On top of the mountain were a few houses, a small sawmill, a store and a post office. It was a quiet community where gentle people lived and worked, digging a living from the stony, yet fertile soil.

The Fentons were a kindhearted couple who had already raised five sons but worked as if all five were still at home. Mrs. Fenton wore long dresses, neatly starched and ironed, even though most women wore their dresses mid-calf. She also kept her gray hair covered with a clean, white kerchief.

Mr. Fenton was tall and slim and wore a full beard the color of salt and pepper. His clean work pants were held up by wide suspenders over a blue chambray shirt. He kept bees and sold the honey.

The Fentons, like most mountain folks, raised all their food. They needed only small amounts of money for staple groceries and kerosene.

Mag waved as she came into the yard.

Mrs. Fenton was on the shady porch, busily knitting. "Look, Jesse, it's Mag Henderson."

Mr. Fenton looked up from his Bible. "Well, hello there, Mag. Get down off your pretty pony and come in the shade. Put your jugs here on the porch and sit a spell. I'll fill the jugs later."

Mag smiled as she slid off the Shetland. "Good afternoon."

Mr. Fenton tugged at his beard. "I'll bet you and the pony could use a cool drink of water."

"Sure could. May I draw it?" Mag enjoyed drawing water. Mrs. Fenton spoke up. "Surely, child. Jesse will be glad for a rest from the well." She chuckled heartily. Mr. Fenton laughed, too. Mag thought their laughter sounded like music.

"Help yourself, child," Mr. Fenton encouraged.

After Mag and Glory had had some fresh water to drink, Mag tied Glory in the shade outside the gate and came to sit by Mrs. Fenton. Mrs. Fenton scooted down to make room for her on the long wooden bench. "How's your folks, honey?"

"Oh, just fine. Daddy's busy with his hay and Mother's canning every day." She giggled at the little rhyme.

Mrs. Fenton laughed and patted Mag's knee. "We've been busy, too. But it will be mighty nice this winter when we reap the rewards of our hot summer's work." Her fingers flew with her knitting. Mag watched fascinated as a heavy, winter sock took shape.

Mr. Fenton asked Mag all about Glory, and she told him that Mr. Henderson would not let her keep the pony.

"Maybe something will happen that your Pa will let you keep her after all."

Mag looked down at her hands. "I'd like that so much." Glory nickered, and they all laughed.

They visited a while. Mag ate two big oatmeal cookies baked that morning and drank a cool glass of goat's milk. The couple took her to see the new baby goats and the spotted pair of mules they had recently bought. The mules would plow the fields. They also would be ridden by the Fentons on their visits to the valley to see their sons and to the village for supplies.

At last Mag said, "I'm really enjoying my visit, but I need to get the honey and head back down the mountain before dark."

"Well, we want you to come back soon." Mr. Fenton took the jugs to the honey house and Mag followed. She loved the smell of the small room he had built especially to extract and store his honey. It reminded her of the candle wax she smelled in church on Sunday, and the honey had a luscious smell all its own. The dark, thick honey ran slowly into the jugs.

"This honey, Mag, is made from many wild flowers. And you see how dark it is? That's because the bees traveled to your Pa's hay fields this spring and feasted there." Mr. Fenton put the corks in securely.

"Goodness, Mr. Fenton, you know all about bees and honey."

He chuckled. "Well, not much, but some, I guess, because I fool with it so much." They walked back to the yard where Mrs. Fenton was waiting with a tiny cloth sack.

"Here, Mag. This is a little bag of lavender leaves I dried. You can put them in the drawer where your Mother stores the linen or your clothes, and they will make everything smell nice."

"Oh, thank you, Mrs. Fenton. I'll enjoy them so much." She held the bag to her nose and inhaled its heavy fragrance. "I love it."

She poked it into her pocket and headed for her pony. "Daddy will settle with you for the honey."

Mr. Fenton placed the honey on the pony. "All right, Mag. Come again soon."

From the simple frame house with all its flowers and herb gardens, the kindly couple waved good-bye. Mag waved back.

She rode a while and then decided to walk. Glory, who seemed unsure of herself going downhill, nickered her thanks.

"You've been such a nice pony today, Glory. When I get home, I'll give you an apple."

Glory seemed to like the idea. To Mag's pleasure, she shook her head up and down. Mag just knew that the pony understood her every word.

A rabbit ran across the narrow road, and Glory only looked. She didn't get spooked as horses often do when something springs in front of them.

Mag laughed suddenly. The rabbit made her think of the skunk family she had seen the other day in the hollow behind the house. There had been a mother and father skunk and three little ones. All five walked in single file. It had reminded the girl of a family out for an afternoon stroll.

Suddenly, she stopped. "Wait, Glory. Look at those pretty pink flowers over there. Mother will love a bouquet for the table." Mag led the pony to a bush where she tied her. She went skipping toward the luscious-smelling flowers, happy to be alive.

Without warning of any kind, Mag felt herself tumbling into darkness. She screamed. Then everything went black.

When Mag came to, she didn't know how long she'd been unconscious. Glory was whinnying continuously.

Mag sat up, groaned and rubbed her head. Her leg hurt. She strained in the half-darkness to see what had happened to it. Her leg was bleeding through her torn pants. "Must have hit a rock when I fell."

She looked around and realized with great fear that she had fallen into an old mine shaft. Lead mines were everywhere in the mountains and some of the old shafts had carelessly been left uncovered. Undergrowth was so thick that it was next to impossible to see the mines before it was too late. In this case, wild roses had covered the opening.

Mag scolded herself. "If I'd just look where I'm going, I wouldn't get into so much trouble." She tried to get to her feet, but her leg hurt when she put weight on it. She finally did stand up, gripping the damp wall. It was a long way to the spot of daylight that glimmered above. Mag shuddered with fear.

"Glory, are you still there?" She hadn't heard the Shetland nicker in a while. "Come over here, Glory. Oh, that won't do. I tied her." She rubbed the bump on her aching head and felt a little blood there, too. She sat back down to ease the pain in her leg.

The shaft led into a mine tunnel. At any other time, the girl might have been excited about such a discovery. She loved caves and enjoyed exploring them with her father. Today, though, alone, hurt and with no light, she felt afraid.

"Surely this is all a bad dream. Maybe I'll wake up soon and find myself in bed." Mag shivered.

She called again, "Glory, say something, girl, so I won't feel scared." But silence was thick in the shaft. "If only I hadn't tied

Without warning of any kind, Mag felt herself tumbling into darkness. She screamed. Then everything went black.

her, she could come and together we might think of something."
She put her head in her hands. "What will I do?"

As she sat there in pain, she began to realize that there *was*
something she could do. She could pray that her folks would find
her.

———————————

Mrs. Henderson looked up the road for what must have
been the tenth time. It was getting late, and she was worried
about her young daughter off on the mountain with the undisciplined Shetland. She scolded herself for allowing Mag to go.

At last, Mrs. Henderson saw the honey-colored Shetland
running wildly down the road, bridle reins flying. No Mag and no
honey jugs were in sight. The mother's heart felt faint as wild
thoughts ran through her mind.

Mr. Henderson was just coming in from the field. Quickly,
his wife told him about Mag. Glory was now standing in front of
them whinnying frantically.

Mr. Henderson flew into a rage. "I told you that fool pony
was no good. Never seen one that was. Now she's thrown Mag
and probably hurt her. I'll beat that crazy filly within an inch of
her life if she's hurt our baby."

"Now Henry, don't say or do anything rash until we find out
what's happened. Let's go up the mountain and see what's
wrong. You know Mag is a level-headed child."

Mr. Henderson ran his hand through his dark hair. "You're
right, honey. I'll go get the truck. See if you can catch that con-
founded Shetland and put her in the barn."

Mrs. Henderson had an idea. "Maybe," she thought,
"maybe the pony is smarter than we think. She just might lead
us to Mag if she is in trouble."

She spoke to Glory. "Do you know where she is, girl? Take us to her." The pony backed away. She didn't trust this woman, even though she spoke kindly.

Mr. Henderson came around with the truck, and his wife got in. The pony ran up the road ahead of the old truck as it struggled and coughed its way up the mountain.

The Shetland-Welsh pony climbed much faster than did the truck. She even stopped to wait for them to catch up with her.

"Well, Henry, have you ever seen such a thing? I wasn't sure the little pony would do it. But will you look—she's leading us to Mag just as sure as the world."

"Well, I'll be a turkey gobbler. I can't believe it. That silly Shetland has done something I didn't think possible. Yes sir, I do believe she's trying to take us to Mag." He frowned. "I hope our girl's all right."

The Hendersons were doing some praying, too.

Mag looked up at the hole. She heard a bobwhite crying. Of course, she knew it was really a quail; "bobwhite" was the name given the bird long ago because of his cry.

The small patch of light above Mag was slowly fading and her fears increased. Yes, night was coming. Now instead of the bobwhite a lonely whippoorwill was crying. Mag pulled the little bag of lavender from her pocket and smelled it again. She looked around her. Bats and all kind of crawly things lived in the caves.... Goose bumps came over her. Mag stood again and cried out with pain. Her leg had swollen a bit now. She hopped directly under the tiny patch of fading light.

"Yelling might not do any good, but here goes anyway." She cupped her hands around her mouth, "Help! Here I am. Please help me, someone!'' It seemed her words were dropping back down into the hole. She shook her head sadly and leaned against the damp wall.

She held her breath, her heart pounding—was that somebody calling? Yes, it was! She heard it again! ''Mag, where are you?'' It was her father's voice.

''Here, Daddy, here I am. Right here.'' She hopped right under the ray of dim light and yelled again: ''Here, Daddy, down in this hole!''

His voice never sounded so good. ''Just stay easy, baby. We're coming. Mother and Glory and I are coming.''

Tears of thanksgiving and relief rolled down her face; God had heard her. Glory nickered and Mag's heart swelled with happiness. The little Shetland had broken loose and gone for help.

Mr. Henderson pointed. ''Mother, she's fallen into the old Turner mine shaft. What was she doing out here?''

Mrs. Henderson was almost in tears. ''She was after those flowers, Henry. I'll bet that's what she was doing over here. And look there, will you. The honey jugs are on the ground, not even broken. I don't know how she managed that.''

Mag's father shook his head. ''I've warned Mag about these shafts. We just allow her too much freedom for her age.''

Mrs. Henderson didn't say anything, but in her heart she knew she had done all she could do with her high-spirited daughter.

They were peering into the hole now but could barely make out the figure below. Glory was trying to see into the hole, too. Down there, Mag didn't even resemble the tangled-haired girl with the long legs.

"Here we are, Mag. Just sit down. I'll go up to the Fentons and get a rope. We'll have you out in no time. Mother will stay here with you."

"All right, Daddy, but please hurry. My leg is hurt and this place gives me the 'willies.'"

Mrs. Henderson was concerned. "Sit down, Honey, off your leg."

Mag sat down right under the hole. "I was trying to get you a bouquet of flowers for the table. Didn't know this old hole was anywhere in the world."

"All right, dear. It's all right."

Mag wiped the tears from her grimy face. "Glory came for you, didn't she? I think that's pretty smart, especially for a *Shetland*."

Mrs. Henderson looked over her shoulder at Mr. Henderson and held back a smile.

He avoided her look and yelled, "Back in a jiff."

The nightmare would soon be over, Mag thought with relief, thanks to the little Shetland that was now pawing the ground.

CHAPTER FIVE

Little Hero

Mag looked around at the beauty of the woods and sighed. It was damp and clean-smelling here and much cooler than going around by the road. "I'm glad we're cutting through these woods to Ruth's house. Aren't you, Glory?" Glory nickered her reply. "And aren't you glad we didn't have to pick those old peas today?" the girl added.

Glory tossed her head, and Mag laughed. "If *you* were going to pick peas, you'd eat them all!" For weeks and weeks the fields were purple with peas. Mag often thought how much easier life would be for her if they would turn the cattle loose and let them eat all of the plants. "But that would be ridiculous," she concluded. "Then we'd be hungry this winter."

Glory picked her way slowly through the branches and around rocks. They were in no hurry, and it was nice here.

Mag pulled the pony to a halt at the brook. The water trickled by slowly. "The brook's almost dry. We could sure use some rain." Many times in early spring she'd seen the same brook gushing noisily over the rocks.

She continued her one-sided conversation, "I hope Ruth's not picking peas today so we can visit. I've only seen her once since school let out." She had missed Ruth. "You know, Glory, we fuss sometimes, but I reckon she's my very best friend."

Glory nibbled at a willow branch which dangled over the little brook.

Mag strained her eyes. "I think I see a big sloe tree over there." Mag loved the plum-like fruit which ripened to a deep blue-black in middle and late summer. "Let's go see, Gal." But just as Mag started to turn the Shetland, Glory reared up on her back legs and the girl went sliding off.

"Glory, what do you think you're doing!" She picked herself up as Glory reared again and whinnied loudly.

"You already threw me, aren't you satisfied? You just wait until I break me a good switch...." Her voice trailed off as she saw with horror the reason for the pony's behavior. A giant cottonmouth lay coiled nearby, ready to strike. Glory was trying her best to trample it.

Chill bumps rippled over Mag, and her green eyes grew big as walnuts. "No, Glory. Come back!" she screamed at the Shetland. "That thing will bite you. Come back!"

Mag tried frantically to reach the reins, but Glory was moving too fast. Down she came, her sharp hooves landing right on top of the snake. The moccasin tightened its coil and struck, thrusting its deadly fangs into the pony's upper leg. Glory whinnied but kept striking away at the enemy.

Now badly hurt, the snake tried only to get clear of those deadly hooves; Glory kept striking until the snake lay very still, and she was sure it was dead.

Mag let out the breath she had been holding for what seemed an eternity and ran to the pony's side. "Glory, you killed it. You saved my life." She was crying and hugging the little Shetland all the while. "And he bit you. I saw him bite you, Glory!" Mag looked down at the spot, which was beginning to swell, and she panicked. She looked into the Shetland's big eyes. Tears were rolling freely down the pony's face. "Oh, Glory, my poor little pony."

Both pony and girl were crying as she took the reins and led the limping Shetland toward home. Mag's only concern was to get the horse home to her father. He would get help. If only Mag had known that the poison spread faster when the animal moved.

Mag brought another armload of fresh hay to the corner of Glory's stall. It was just something to do; she knew the pony would not eat. Mag couldn't bear to see Glory all stretched out in the corner of the barn lying so still.

The young vet leaned over Glory and frowned. He spoke in low tones so Mag wouldn't hear. "Mr. Henderson, if only your daughter had left the little thing and come for help. The poison's surely all through her system by now. Even though I've given her everything I know of, I don't see how she can make it." He pushed his glasses up on his nose and sighed.

Mr. Henderson squatted by the veterinarian. "Well, it's not our horse. Belongs to a friend. We're just keeping her until he sells her or comes for her this fall."

The doctor looked surprised. "Oh, the way your daughter was acting, I thought it was hers."

Mr. Henderson looked uncomfortable. "Well, unfortunately, Mag has taken a liking to Glory even though I warned her it couldn't stay here. I don't have a bit of use for a small horse." He pulled his pipe from his shirt pocket. "I told her not to get too fond of it."

The doctor looked at Mr. Henderson a moment and then back at Glory. "Well, only a miracle will save this little thing. She probably will give her life after having saved your daughter's."

Mr. Henderson had a faraway look on his lean face. "Yes, I guess you're right." He was remembering the mine shaft incident. "She's turning into a regular little hero." He wished he could change his attitude toward ponies.

Mag came back with more hay and spoke to the doctor. "Will she be all right?" The question tugged at her heart.

The gentle doctor looked up at the girl. "Honey, she's a mighty sick pony. I've done everything I can for her."

Mag knew he hadn't answered her question, but she didn't want him to say more. Her heart had never hurt her so. She wondered if it was breaking in two.

The girl squatted beside Glory and wiped the pony's tears. "Did you ever see a horse cry like that?" she asked the vet. "Glory always cries when her feelings are hurt or something hurts her."

Mr. Henderson started to say something but decided to listen.

The doctor looked interested. "No, Mag, can't say that I have. Horses have tears for washing the eyes when an object gets in them, but never have I seen one cry." The kindly man saw no reason for telling her that he didn't think horses really cried, but he was wondering himself why the tears kept coming back when there was nothing in the Shetland's eyes. It was something he planned to look up in his medical books. "I do hope she gets well, Mag," he added thoughtfully.

Mag thanked him and sat down beside the pony. Everyone left the barn so that Mag and Glory were alone.

Later in the evening, Mrs. Henderson gently opened the barn door and peeked in at her daughter. "Does the lantern need oil, Mag?"

Mag looked up at her mother, startled by her presence. "I think there's plenty. I filled it earlier." She looked into her mother's face. "Glory's not a bit better, is she?"

Her mother knelt beside her. "Well, she doesn't look any worse either. Maybe it will take some time for the doctor's medicine to work."

Mag nodded and reached for the pan of water to offer it to Glory, but the pony paid no attention.

Mrs. Henderson whispered, "I'm going back to the house. Don't you want to come, too, and get a little rest?"

Mag showed surprise. "I can't leave her by herself, Mother. I'll just rest here beside her, if it's all right with you."

Mrs. Henderson nodded and smiled. "I'll be back later and see how she is."

Mag looked up at the loft of the big old barn. How many fun times she'd had playing in the hay. Gazing upward, Mag just naturally thought of the One who could make her pony well, and she spoke to Him:

"It seems like I've been begging you so long, God, but I just can't stop. When I keep begging Mother, she gives in *sometimes*. Other times, though, she gets angry if I keep begging and she won't let me have what I want. But I just can't stop asking and begging." She paused and lifted herself up onto her knees. "Glory saved my life, you know. I probably won't get to keep her, but maybe if you let her live, some other little girl will be able to enjoy her. I know Glory is ornery and stubborn sometimes, but I love her so. I just couldn't bear it if she died. Please, God, please!"

She lay down and placed her head next to Glory's and sobbed herself to sleep. In her dream, Mag saw Glory, but the Shetland was much taller. Mag was mounted on her, but the girl's feet were a long way from the ground. Suddenly Mag woke up.

Running to the door, she yelled with all her might: "Mother, Daddy, come see!"

Something was nibbling at her ear. Her heart was pounding as she opened her eyes. There was Glory...on her feet!

Mag scrambled up almost bursting at the seams with happiness. She looked at the pony's leg. It was still somewhat swollen, but Mag knew that the poison had done all the harm it was going to. "Glory! Oh, Glory! You're going to be all right!" Running to the door, she yelled with all her might: "Mother, Daddy, come see!"

Mr. Henderson scratched his head. "Well, I'll be a cat's uncle. I believe she's going to be all right, Mag." Mag thought she saw his hand move toward Glory, but maybe she didn't. He had never touched the pony.

Mrs. Henderson rubbed Glory's neck. "Oh, little pony, you're better and that's just wonderful."

Mr. Henderson opened the barn door and the sunshine rushed in. "That vet really knows his business," he remarked.

Mag looked at her father and smiled. She knew that the vet was good, all right, but she also knew the real, honest-to-goodness reason Glory was going to be well, and she thanked God for the favor. Then she gave Glory's neck a squeeze and brought fresh water, which the pony drank freely.

CHAPTER SIX

Ripe Peaches

Mag and Glory poked along the gravel road on their way to the McAlister peach orchard. Mag's parents had allowed her to ride ahead on Glory since it was only a mile or so to the orchard. Glory nibbled at grass along the way. Mag knew this wasn't good for the undisciplined pony, but it was too hot to hurry.

Mag and her mother had washed fruit jars the day before. Now the jars stood shiny-bright on the big table waiting for the ripe fruit to be packed inside. The filled jars would then be taken to the wood-burning stove and cooked before being stored away for winter. Mag's mouth watered as she thought of the dishes of golden peaches covered with heavy cream, and of the pies and cobblers her mother would make with the fruit. Mag rubbed the pony's neck. "I guess it's worth all the peach-picking," she said to Glory.

The pony pricked up her ears and nickered. As they neared the orchard, they saw several cars and pickup trucks and a wagon.

The peach orchard covered several acres. Mr. McAlister allowed his neighbors to pick the peaches each year, asking only a small sum per bushel. Many in the community were there to take advantage of his generous offer.

"There's my cotton-haired friend, Ruth." Mag waved. "It's almost a fun thing when so many people are here, Glory." Mag slid off the pony and tied her to a fence post before running to greet her friend.

The orchard was snuggled between mountains, so it would be a while before the sun climbed high enough to be uncomfortable. The crew of peach-pickers was grateful for that.

"Hi, Mag." Ruth was slight of figure and not as tall as Mag.

"Hi, yourself." They talked for a while before Ruth went to join her family.

Mr. and Mrs. Henderson soon came chug-a-lugging along in the old truck. Her parents began unloading the baskets, and Mag lifted them over the fence. "It's cool in the orchard, Mother."

Mrs. Henderson adjusted her hat. "It surely is. If we hurry, we might get done before the sun finds us."

Mr. Henderson walked toward the gate. "Won't take long to get ours filled." He winked at Mag.

Mr. Henderson picked up a basket. "Mother, why don't you and Mag pick from the same tree, and I'll get the one next to you."

She nodded, and they went to a tree that was loaded with fruit. Mag wished she could pick from the same tree as Ruth, but there was no need to ask. Their folks knew how the girls giggled when they were together; they wouldn't get very many peaches picked that way. Still, there would be short rest periods when the two could visit, and that suited the girls just fine.

Since peaches bruise easily when ripe, Mag was very careful. Her mouth watered for a piece of the juicy fruit, but she couldn't bear the fuzzy peel. She'd have to wait until they were served; then her mother would let her have her fill.

She reached over her head and plucked peach after peach, placing them gently in the basket. Soon her arms were tired.

Mag wondered why grown-ups didn't get tired. Her mother seemed as fresh as when they had started.

Mr. McAlister furnished ladders, and the taller people picked the fruit that was high off the ground. The orchard was a busy place.

Mrs. Henderson already had filled one basket. Mr. Henderson came down from his ladder and carried it to the truck.

Glory whinnied. She was lonely and tired of being tied to a fence. Mag looked in her direction. "I wish you could pick, too. My arms are tired." An idea flashed into her mind. She walked over to the fence and untied the pony. Then she brought it back to the tree and mounted. Quietly, she said, "Now, you just stand still, and I won't have to reach so far over my head. This will be much easier sitting down."

All went well until Mrs. Henderson came back with an empty basket and discovered them. She cried out in astonishment: "Mag, what on earth are you doing with that pony in this orchard. Take her out at once!"

That was a mistake. Mrs. Henderson's agitated voice and movements frightened Glory, and the pony shot off through the orchard at breakneck speed. Mag's hair got caught in the tree, yanking her off the pony. The next thing Mag knew she was on the ground, and Glory was flying through the orchard, scattering filled baskets of fruit in every direction. Everyone began to yell at her—another mistake, since it excited the Shetland even more.

Mag ran after Glory as fast as her long legs would carry her, yelling and pleading for the pony to come back. On and on Glory went. Mag felt sick to her stomach.

Mr. and Mrs. Henderson ran, too, trying to catch the runaway pony. Exhausted, Glory stopped at one end of the orchard and stared at her pursuers.

Mag ran up and grabbed the bridle. She was almost completely out of breath. "I'm so mad I could whip you good, Glory," she gasped.

Mr. Henderson came up behind her. He was very upset, but to Mag's surprise he was angrier at her than at the pony. "Mag, how could you do such a foolish thing? Get that pony out of this orchard. We'll have to pick up all these folks' fruit, which is bruised now, and then stay up half the night picking up our own."

He glared at his young daughter, who just put her head down. Mr. Henderson turned away and looked at the scene.

Tears came pouring from Mag's eyes. She was feeling pretty sorry for herself. Why didn't her father understand how a ten-year-old kid feels? She led the pony outside the orchard and tied her once more to the fence. The pickers silently watched as the pony was led out. Then, without another word, everyone pitched in and picked up the spilled fruit and overturned baskets.

Mag came back and said in a loud voice, "I'm sorry, everybody." She couldn't bear for them to be angry with her and Glory.

Her apology, so sincere, broke the ice. Everyone said it was all right. Ruth came over. "It's all right, Mag. We can just eat more now."

Mag looked at her friend fondly and smiled. "Thank you."

Later, as she put Glory in the barn, she talked to her as usual, "At least you could *act* sorry that you made such a mess."

The filly nibbled at her hair. "You are sorry, I know that." She hugged the pony, remembering what her parents had said to her about shortcuts often being more trouble than they are worth. "I'm afraid you're making it harder for me to convince Daddy that you should stay with us." She rubbed the pony's neck. "Maybe you can think up something fantastic to make up for it." She liked the sound of the word "fantastic" and decided to use it again. "Wouldn't it be fantastic if you found some hidden treasure?" Glory nickered and then picked at a tuft of grass growing just outside the barn.

Mag was in one of her dream worlds. "Yes, that would be simply fan..."

Her mother's call brought her back to reality. "Come along, Mag. Let's get started on these peaches." Both parents were still a little upset with her, and Mag didn't want to do anything to rile them further.

She turned to Glory on her way out. "You ought to be glad you're a horse so you don't have to peel a million bushels of peaches, most of them bruised, thanks to you."

Glory only nodded her head up and down.

CHAPTER SEVEN

The Haunted House

"Ruth, do you ever wish you were a boy?" The two girls were on their way to the post office at Shiloh. Mag was riding Glory, and Ruth was on the family horse, Major.

"No, I sure don't."

"Well, don't you wish we could do the things Tom Sawyer and Huckleberry Finn did, like build a raft and float down the Mississippi River?" Mag played with Glory's mane as she talked.

"That was just a made-up story." Ruth shooed a fly away from Major's ear.

"I'll bet there are boys who have done that."

"Maybe, but I sure don't want to build a raft and float down the river. I'd rather be on Major heading for the post office on top of the mountain to see if the fall catalogs have come in yet. So, there."

"Oh, Ruth, you just don't have a bit of imagination. You're so...." She couldn't think of the right word so she left her sentence hanging.

"I don't care. I like being me."

Mag tried to explain. "I guess I'm glad I'm a girl, but it seems boys can do so many more exciting things than girls."

Ruth put her free hand on her hip. "I don't know how you can think that, Mag Henderson. You cause enough excitement for the whole mountain."

They laughed and Mag tossed her long, tangled hair. "Say, Ruth, let's ride down by the old Thurman Place and see if there's really money buried there like people say."

"Mag Henderson, are you trying to get us killed? What are you going to dig in the rocks with, your bare hands?" Ruth shook her head in disbelief. "Besides, that place is haunted!" Her voice squeaked with excitement.

"You don't really believe that," Mag said with a frown. "And anyway, if it looks promising, we could come back with a pick."

"Yes, I believe it. I've heard some spooky tales about that old place."

"That's because it's been vacant so long. It'll be fun to go by there and look around. Besides, we're too early for the mail. We'd just have to stand around and wait."

Ruth sighed. Mag knew she was giving in.

"Okay, Mag, but just for a minute, and remember, if it was dark, you couldn't *pay* me to go near the Thurman Place."

"Well, I wouldn't care if it was dark or not."

The steep road was rough, and as the horses picked their way around, Mag had to hold her feet high to keep from stubbing her toes on some of the big rocks.

The road ended and only a faint trail was visible. The horses were having trouble walking the downhill part, so Mag and Ruth got down and led them. The girls had been going barefoot all summer and could hardly feel the many small rocks.

They looked up as a cloud covered the hot sun. Ruth spoke. "Wish some rain would come out of that big old cloud and cool things off." She fanned herself. Soon, thunder rumbled through the mountains. It seemed to go on forever. "I believe it *is* fixing to rain, Mag. We'd best go back."

"We will in a minute. There's the house. Come on."

At one time, it had been a fine structure, but years of use and then of vacancy had left their mark. It sagged at its foundations, looking very lonely.

Ruth didn't like the looks of it. "Wonder what happened to the people who used to live there. I've heard tell they were murdered and buried in the cellar."

Mag stopped and put her hand on her hip. "You believe that junk, too, I suppose. Mother says they were elderly. I imagine they went to live with some of their grown children."

Ruth wrinkled her nose at Mag. "They still might be in the cellar."

Mag ignored her remark and said dreamily, "It must have been a beautiful place. Just look at that picket fence and those fireplace chimneys."

Ruth caught her mood. "And look at the big porch. I'll bet that little old lady sat on it many an afternoon in a high-backed rocker." She shook her head sadly. "Now, it is almost rotted down at one end."

The thunder rumbled louder and lightning flashed. A few drops of rain began to fall.

Ruth came out of her dreamy mood in a hurry. "Let's go, Mag. We've seen it." She started to mount.

Mag pleaded, "Wait, Ruth. Just another minute. I want to look inside." She started up the steps.

"Well, you better look in a hurry or we'll be soaking wet."

"I just want to peek inside," Mag repeated. She walked up on the porch and stuck her head through the paneless window. "Nobody's home." She laughed at her joke.

A great flash of lightning crackled across the sky. Ruth was fast losing her patience. "Hurry, Mag, let's go!"

Before she had time to say more, the rain started to come down in sheets. Ruth jumped up on the porch. "Now we're in trouble!"

Mag consoled her. "That's all right. We have a nice shelter. Let's bring the horses on the porch. Seems sturdy enough at this end."

Ruth swallowed hard. "We're going *inside?*"

"Sure, why not? Looks dry."

They coaxed the horses onto the porch. The animals stood there feeling insecure, but seemingly glad to be out of the driving rain. Glory nudged Mag with her nose. "It's all right, girl. You'll be fine. Just stand still."

Mag looked at Ruth, who stood with her arms folded and her eyes wide open. "Well, let's go inside."

Ruth frowned and made a dreadful face. "Well, maybe just a *little* ways inside."

"You don't want to get wet, do you? Come on in." Mag was already inside of the big living room with its high ceilings and long windows.

"Well, I'd just about as soon be wet as scared to death."

"Silly. Let's just sit down and wait for the rain to stop." Mag found a chair with three legs and pretended to sit on it. "Oops! Dear me, this chair just must be repaired very soon." She giggled. Her relaxed manner was catching. Ruth began to peek inside a closet and into a great hall.

Suddenly, they thought they heard a sound in the back part of the house. Ruth's eyes grew to the size of saucers. "What was that?" She clutched Mag's shoulder. "Did you hear it?"

Mag was a bit frightened, but she refused to let Ruth know. "Probably a broken shutter flapping in the wind. Let's go take a look."

Mag was a bit frightened, but she refused to let Ruth know. "Probably a broken shutter flapping in the wind. Let's go take a look."

"Take a look? Not in a million years." Ruth folded her arms again.

"Then stay here, and I'll go look." She started down the hall.

"Wait, I'll go with you."

Ruth stayed close behind Mag as they crept down the long hall and back to the kitchen area. Mag pushed open a heavy door. It creaked painfully.

Both girls swallowed hard.

A strange looking contraption almost filled the large kitchen area. It resembled a boiler of sorts with pipes coming from it. Barrels and gallon jugs and jars were all over the floor.

Ruth found her voice first. "What's *that?*"

Mag sniffed. "I'm not sure, but that smell reminds me of the stuff Mother gives me for a bad cold."

Ruth sniffed.

Mag nodded slowly. "That thing's probably a whiskey still."

Ruth started to panic. "It's against the law to make whiskey."

Mag whistled long and low. "You can just bet it's against the law."

"Well, let's get ourselves out of here. The moonshiners might be around." Now Ruth was shaking. "They might even be in the cellar."

"Yeah, they might be. We better hit the road and fast."

The rain pelted down on the tin roof of the kitchen and made such a noise the girls had to yell to hear each other. Mag gave one last look at the still. It didn't seem to be in operation now. "They won't likely come out in the rain, unless they're already here."

Suddenly, a loud scream pierced the air. Both girls felt chill bumps race from toe to scalp. They ran to the front of the house, quickly led their horses down from the porch and, despite the pouring rain, mounted them. In seconds they were drenched, but neither one noticed it.

They coaxed their horses up the hill. The rain was blinding.

Mag's hair was in strings and Ruth's was plastered to her head. They kept looking back over their shoulders, expecting to see whatever had screamed looming right behind them.

Just before reaching the road, they met a rider in a black slicker suit. Their hearts nearly stopped. He was heading for the Thurman Place.

When his horse reached theirs, he stopped, but the girls kept their eyes straight ahead and tried to keep going.

He yelled to them: "What are you kids doing out in this storm?" His voice was scratchy like radio static.

Mag called an excuse over her shoulder. It seemed to satisfy the rider. He nodded and continued picking his way down the hill toward the house.

When Mag and Ruth were out of his hearing, Ruth spoke shakily, "That was Skit Rudney, sure as the world. He's already been in prison for moonshining and I'll bet he's back at it at that very house." She pointed a shaky finger back toward the house.

"Well, we're lucky to have gotten away when we did," Mag said. "He's going to know we were there and might come looking for us."

"Yeah, I imagine we left wet tracks." Ruth sighed heavily. "I knew I shouldn't have listened to you, Mag Henderson. Now we're really in a heap of trouble."

Mag agreed and the girls encouraged their horses to hurry. "What do you suppose screamed?" Mag wondered.

Ruth insisted, "The place is haunted, I told you."

"No such thing. Either a person or a mountain lion screamed. Mountain lions sound a lot like women when they scream."

Ruth wasn't satisfied. "Well, a mountain lion wouldn't be inside the house, would it?"

"Might not have been. The scream might have come from the edge of the woods behind the house."

"Might, might, might. It *might* have come from that lady buried in the cellar, too."

Mag eyed her friend. "You sure are upset."

The rain had all but stopped by the time the girls reached the post office and picked up the mail and the fall catalogs. They didn't mention the still or the mysterious rider to anyone at the post office but hurried home to tell their folks.

The young constable came into the Henderson's yard riding a white Morgan horse. Mag was brushing Glory. "Where's your daddy?" he asked.

"In the house. You want to see him about the still?"

He smiled. "I do, young lady, but I want to speak to your father *and* you."

She nodded and started toward the house, but her father walked out on the porch to greet the lawman.

"Good morning, Mr. Henderson," the constable said. "I came as soon as I got your message about the still at the old Thurman Place."

"Yes, well the girls had no business being there, but they stumbled onto it. From what they tell me, it isn't in operation right now. It's a wonder some of those moonshiners weren't there though; they could have harmed the girls." Mr. Henderson frowned at Mag. He was still upset that they had placed themselves in such danger.

Mag lowered her head. She didn't like to displease her father. She felt ashamed.

Glory nickered. She wanted Mag to continue brushing her.

The constable scratched his head. "Well, since they didn't come to any harm, I'm mighty glad they found it. It's a little too close to the road to make whiskey; maybe the thing is just in storage there." He rubbed his clean-shaven chin. "Then again, they might just want me to think that. They probably think I don't know my hat from the end of a plow, but I plan to mess up their little scheme."

Mr. Henderson looked at the dark-haired constable. "You might be right about them trying to throw you off the track."

"Yes, well, the reason for my visit is to ask you to keep your daughter close at home for a while. She can identify that Rudney fellow, and I might have to use her as a witness. We want to be sure she will be safe."

Mag swallowed hard. She hadn't thought of that. Surely, Rudney wouldn't harm a kid...or would he? "What about Ruth? She saw him going there, too."

"I was just going over to tell Mr. Johnson the same thing I've told your father, Mag. No need to hide; just stay close and don't wander off alone."

Mag nodded. Mr. Henderson walked over and put his arm around her shoulder and squeezed it. "I'll see that she doesn't wander off." His arm made her feel safe. Mag had no intention of going very far. No intention at all.

"I'll be back in touch, Mr. Henderson." The constable mounted his beautiful horse. Glory was very glad he was leaving; she didn't like strange horses in her territory.

As soon as the lawman left, Mrs. Henderson hurried into the yard. Mag knew that her mother was upset. "Mag, I was listening from inside the house. I want you to do *exactly* as the constable said."

"Yes, Mother, I will." She picked up the brush and led Glory to the pasture. "Boy, what a miserable mess I'm into now."

Glory whinnied loudly in agreement.

CHAPTER EIGHT

The Peddler

Even though Mag was "grounded" for a while, there was plenty to do and see around the farm. She brought Glory to the edge of the clearing. A rustle in the trees caught her attention. It was a magnificent deer. "A six-point buck," Mag told herself. Her eyes grew wide. She could have stood there forever.

From the porch, Mrs. Henderson's voice rang out: "Mag, come on now. I'm ready for your help." The deer leaped high into the air. It landed on a nearby ledge and disappeared into the woods.

"All right, Mother," the girl answered. Reluctantly, she turned back. Glory was glad to be returning to her pasture.

Mag put the pony in the pasture behind the barn and joined her mother in the yard.

"I've finished the apples and I want you to water the chickens. But first, young lady, sit down here and let me comb your hair. I want to get every last tangle out and braid it nicely."

"Oh, Mother."

"Not another word, Mag. You haven't combed your hair well since church time Sunday and here it is the middle of the week." Her voice was pleasant but firm. Mag knew when she had lost. She walked across the yard and sat on a little stool in front of her mother and sighed.

"What were you looking at when I called you?"

"I was watching a big buck. When you called, you scared him away. Ouch, that hurts."

"I'm sorry. There seem to be quite a lot of deer this year. Daddy says that's a good sign."

Mag had heard him say it many times.

Mrs. Henderson tied the last braid with a red ribbon, then both of them heard someone coming down the mountain.

"Mercy, Mag, that sounds like the peddler. I hope so." She got up from her chair and went into the house to put the comb away.

Mag jumped up from her stool and ran to greet the peddler.

The peddler visited the community twice a year in his old rattle-trap truck. He sharpened scissors, axes, knives and saws and repaired pots and pans. He sold a variety of little things like vanilla extract, thread, needles, pencils, tablets, etc. In addition, he was one of the most interesting persons Mag had ever known.

"Hello, Mr. Prattleworth." She ran beside his truck.

The small man stopped and got out. "Hello, Mag and Mrs. Henderson. It's good to see you once again."

Mrs. Henderson smiled as he lifted his hat and bowed low. There was not a single hair on his smooth head. "Mr. Prattleworth, I'm very glad to see you, too," Mag's mother began. "I have lots of work for you. Mr. Henderson's been so busy with the hay, he hasn't had time to sharpen a single thing. I'm all out of vanilla extract and black thread, too. Could have gone to the village, but I wanted to wait for you."

Mag was glad her mother was like that.

"You're all kindness, Mrs. Henderson, and I appreciate your thoughtfulness most highly."

Mag thought Mr. Prattleworth must be an educated man. He spoke with such manners and seemed to be a real gentleman.

He took out his tools and strange looking boxes. Mag was spellbound by all the things he pulled from the old truck. He had a wooden frame built on the back of the truck. Pots and pans hung from the frame, along with other things he had picked up in exchange for his work when folks had no money. He even had a cage of several squawking chickens, a bucket of big red apples and another bucket filled with potatoes.

Mag couldn't wait to tell Mr. Prattleworth about the pony. She pulled her little stool as close as she could without being in his way while he set up his work area. "I'll bet you've never seen a half Shetland and half Welsh pony, have you?"

The little man scratched his head. His eyes were the color of green maypops. "Half Shetland and half Welsh, eh?" He began mending one of the pots Mag's mother had brought him. "Can't say I have, but I did see a Connemara pony once."

Mag thought he was teasing and laughed. "A what?"

"A Connemara. No joke. They come from a place called Connemara on the west coast of Ireland."

Mag was interested. Meanwhile, Mrs. Henderson went in and out of the house; soon Mr. Prattleworth's workbench was full.

"Yessiree," the peddler remarked, "that part of Ireland is a rugged, rocky place where ponies must really forage for a living. And because they're used to the mountainous terrain, they're mighty sure-footed little things. They naturally take to jumping." He held the pot between him and the sun to see if the hole had sealed. "They're bigger than a Shetland and come in all colors. The one I saw was on a farm in Virginia. It was dun-colored with a black mane and tail."

Mag sighed. She wished she could see all the things Mr. Prattleworth had seen. "Well, the Con...whatever you called it, sounds nice, but I guess my little Shetland-Welsh will do me."

Mrs. Henderson brought some knives to be sharpened. "Now, Honey, your father hasn't said he'd buy Glory; so don't go saying she's *yours.*"

Mag looked quickly at her mother. She had forgotten that she might not be able to keep Glory forever. A feeling of sadness crept into her heart for a moment even though Mr. Prattleworth was here and was about to start with his funny stories.

He looked at Mag with kindness and said, "I hope you can keep your pony, Mag."

She nodded. "Me, too."

He laughed to himself suddenly. "Say, did I tell you the story about the snake that bit the hoe handle?"

Mag smiled. She heard it every time he came, but she never tired of it. "Please tell it."

"Well, this old cottonmouth snake was going along one day minding his business, and he met this hoe leaning against the wall of the barn where some tired farmer had left it. Mr. Snake spoke to the hoe. When the hoe didn't speak back, Mr. Snake was quite put out and thought that the hoe was very rude. 'Maybe he didn't hear me.' He spoke again, and still the hoe just kept leaning against the barn. Now, Mr. Snake didn't like to be ignored, so he just bit the handle real hard until all the poison he could muster was inside the handle. 'Now, how do you like that?' Still, the hoe handle didn't speak. The snake went back into the woods mumbling to himself.

"Well, sir, that hoe handle began to swell from all that terrible poison, mind you, and it kept on swelling until it was the size of a big tree log. Mr. Farmer came along to finish working in the garden. He began looking for his hoe, but then he saw the log, which of course was really the hoe. 'That looks like my hoe,' and sure enough, when he ran around to the other end, there was the little metal blade so far down in the wood he could hardly see it."

Mag, her elbows on her knees, was wiggling with happy anticipation. Mrs. Henderson sat nearby knitting and smiling to herself.

" 'My,' said the farmer, 'what could have happened to my hoe? Well, it's too big to use for a hoe so I'll just take it down to the sawmill and have it sawed into lumber and build something with it.' "

Mag giggled. The idea of such a thing happening made her laugh. This pleased Mr. Prattleworth. He stood up, using both hands to elaborate his story.

"Why, after it was sawed, the farmer had a plumb wagon-load full of fine lumber, and he built a nice hog pen and put twenty-five hogs inside to fatten up for market."

Then Mr. Prattleworth made a wry face. "Well, sir, a terrible thing happened. The next day, the swelling began to go down in that handle and the pen began to shrink and the hogs were squealing and choking, and the farmer had to turn the hogs out. He stood looking as the pen just got smaller and smaller." Mr. Prattleworth suddenly snapped his fingers, "And Bingo! It was just an ordinary skinny hoe handle once more lying there.

"Well, Mr. Farmer was completely dismayed and thoroughly aggravated and declared to his wife, Mrs. Farmer, that never again would he leave his hoe standing by the garden fence or against the barn. He would finish his job and put the hoe in the toolshed where it belonged, so no more snakes could bite it and cause all that unnecessary work. And that's what he did, all right." Mr. Prattleworth sat down.

Mag clapped her hands. "That's a very funny story, Mr. Prattleworth. Tell another one."

Mrs. Henderson smiled. "Now, Mag, I need you to help me get lunch started. Pretty soon your daddy will be coming in from the field, and Mr. Prattleworth will be getting hungry, too."

"You're a very kind lady, Mrs. Henderson," the peddler said with a nod. "I always look forward to your fine meals each time I'm in these parts. And Mag, I'd be mighty pleased to see that fine pony later on today."

Mag smiled at him. Nodding happily, she skipped up the steps into the house.

That afternoon, Mag helped her mother prepare supper. The girl was hungry, and the fried chicken and blueberry muffins looked mighty good.

As Mrs. Henderson stirred flour into the iron skillet to make gravy, she said, "Mag, see how much more Mr. Prattleworth has to do and tell him supper's just about ready."

"All right."

Mag looked longingly at the platter of golden brown chicken and then at her mother, who shook her head and smiled, "Not until supper. Your daddy will be here soon."

Mag shrugged her shoulders and walked into the yard. Mr. Prattleworth was putting his tools back into the truck and humming a cheery little tune. He turned and smiled at Mag, "Well, young lady, I'm all finished here. Want to show me that fine pony now?"

"I'd love to, but won't you stay for supper? We're having fried chicken and blueberry muffins."

"Sounds mighty fine, but that lunch your mother fixed will hold me quite a while yet. I want to make it to Plainesville before dark." He wiped his hands and looked toward the sun.

"Oh, well, let me introduce you to Glory," Mag said.

They walked to the pasture gate, and Mag called, "Come here, Glory." The pony looked up but went back to grazing.

"Glory, you had better come here," Mag tried again. The Shetland didn't even bother to look up that time.

"Never mind, Mag. Let her eat," Mr. Prattleworth said. "I can see her from here. She's beautiful all right. I hope everything works out for you to keep her. But you'll be wanting a bigger horse before long." The kind little man with twinkling eyes patted Mag on the head. "I'll bet by the time I come back, you'll be a head taller."

She smiled. "I guess I will need a larger horse, but I want Glory."

He gave her a sympathetic look. "I can understand that. Ponies have a special kind of personality. By the way, do you know how a pony is classified?"

Mag shook her head.

"Aside from the difference in general appearance, a horse and pony differ in height. A pony is fourteen hands and two inches. Anything taller than that is no longer called a pony, but a horse."

"Daddy said a hand is four inches."

"That's right, but I'll bet you don't know how this hand measuring business got started."

No, Mag didn't know that.

"Long ago, the King of England, Henry VIII, had a serious dislike for 'little horses' as ponies were then called."

Mag nodded. "Just like Daddy."

Mr. Prattleworth propped his foot on the fence railing and continued, "He wanted all the animals to be great war horses. The king issued a decree—that means he passed a law—that any stallion under fourteen hands would be in danger of being destroyed if it were found. In some places the limit was about fifteen hands, so a happy medium was arrived at: fourteen hands and two inches."

"That old king was sure mean to destroy all those beautiful little horses," Mag remarked.

Mr. Prattleworth continued, "Fortunately, some small stallions were hidden out in the moors, so even today there are many small breeds of ponies in Great Britain."

"Gosh, Mr. Prattleworth, how do you know so many things?"

He smiled, "I don't know that much, honey. But what I do know I've learned from reading and travel. You know, travel is the very best kind of education. Just take notice of the things and people you see while you're moving about and ask a few questions now and then."

"You could be a teacher or something instead of a..." Mag paused. She didn't know the proper name of his trade.

"A drummer, or some say a peddler?" Mr. Prattleworth looked off into the distance. "I could have, but I have this itching in my feet, and it just won't let me stay put. Besides, I'm happier at this trade than anything else I've tried—and I've tried a lot of things." The good man chuckled and put his hands into his pockets. "No matter what a man's trade, if it gives him satisfaction, he'll be happy, and his job will have a certain dignity to it."

Mag thought about that for a moment. "I think it's nice that you like your work. My daddy loves being a hay and cattle farmer, although he says there's not much profit in it."

"Yes, your father is a contented man. And with you and your mother thrown in for good measure, how could he be otherwise?"

Mag smiled at the happy little man. Together they looked at Glory, who was still grazing.

"She's a fine little pony, Mag."

"Thank you. I know they're strong animals. Little as Glory is, she's really strong. But what are some ponies you can ride when you get too long-legged, like I'm getting?" She sighed.

"There's a long list of ponies that adults ride. There's the Connemara I told you about. He's about fourteen hands high, where your pony looks about ten or eleven hands to me. Then, you have your crossbreeds; that's when a big mare is crossed with a small Shetland stallion or vice-versa.

"Then, there are the ponies from Iceland. They stand about thirteen-and-a-half hands high and are very, very sturdy and strong. They are also gentle. Adults ride them all the time. But ponies from Iceland haven't been imported into this country. You see, they couldn't be put in barns or stables. They have to be left outside where they naturally do better, being used to cold and all; they can't stand heat. If I had a hankering for a pony, that's the kind I'd get."

"But I could never get one of those," Mag said sadly.

The peddler looked surprised. "Don't say *never.* It sounds too final. Always think that someday you will be able to do such and such a thing. And if you want it badly enough, you *will* be able to do it or have it. Remember, there's always a way."

They were walking back to the truck when Mrs. Henderson came out on the porch. She talked a few minutes with the peddler and paid him for his day's work.

Mag hated to see him leave—this strange, yet wonderful little man. He had made her day brighter, and she had learned so much from him. She watched him as he got into his old truck that had tools, pots and pans hanging from its sides.

"Thank you again, Mrs. Henderson, for the fine meal and the work. See you in a few months. Good-bye, Mag."

They waved to Mr. Prattleworth as he drove away in his old truck—pots and pans banging and crated chickens squawking.

CHAPTER NINE

A Carnival Pony

The empty pasture caused Mag's heart to ache just like a bad sore. How could her daddy have done it? She had come back from Ruth's house—the only place she was allowed to go besides church until the moonshiners were caught. When she had looked for Glory, the pony was gone! Mr. Roarks had come for her unexpectedly and had sold her to someone.

Mag now sat at the kitchen table, the pieces of a puzzle spread out before her. She looked through the window and watched the water run down the rain pipe. It was a good soaking rain and everyone was grateful. Lately, gardens had been dry and wells low of water.

"I wonder what she's doing right now," Mag wondered aloud.

"Who, dear?" Mrs. Henderson looked up from her magazine.

"Glory. I hope whoever bought her will be good to her."

"I'm sure they will." She looked into her daughter's face. "Mag, I wish we could have convinced your daddy to let her stay, but he's a very prideful man. It would be quite difficult for him to admit that he was wrong, particularly when his feelings are so strong about small horses."

Mag was really trying to understand.

Mrs. Henderson continued, "I know he feels bad about it though. He told me he wants to look around for a big horse for you."

Mag frowned and remarked, "Just like King Henry." When her mother looked puzzled, Mag said, "Please tell Pa not to be in a hurry, because I don't *want* a big horse." She went to her room.

Mrs. Henderson shook her head sadly and went back to her magazine.

———————————

A small carnival was coming to the village. Mag and Ruth were excited.

"It will be so much fun to see the animals and ride the ferris wheel, won't it, Mag? And eat cotton candy?" Ruth whirled around in excitement.

"Yes, and I like the candy apples and hot dogs, too." Mag was trying to be strong even though she missed Glory. After all, she had been warned time and time again that she could not keep the pony, and there was no need to be sad forever. But her heart tugged painfully when she thought of the honey-colored Shetland.

"Do you think we can go to the carnival together, Ruth?"

"I guess so. My family's going tonight, too. We can walk around together. Since our folks will be right there, we'll be safe. Sure wish the constable would let us know about the moonshiners."

"Me, too," Mag sighed. "It's weird thinking they might try to hurt us."

"We'll be safe if we stick together," Ruth said. "Can't wait till tonight. See you then."

Mag was fascinated with the little carnival. She loved the music of the merry-go-round, the booming voices of the barkers and the wonderful smell of roasted peanuts, popcorn and cotton candy. Even the sawdust under her feet had a special smell.

The girls watched with open mouths while a big man wearing a white turban swallowed a flaming sword.

"How does he do that?" Ruth was dumbfounded.

"There's got to be a trick to it," Mag said matter-of-factly. "He's no different from anyone else; it would cut him and burn him, too."

"Yeah, I guess so, but he's sure good at it."

Soon the two girls had spent all their money, but they were happy just walking around, enjoying the sights and sounds of the carnival, watching all the happy folks who had gathered there.

Suddenly, Mag stopped. "Look, Ruth, they have a pony ride. Let's go over and watch."

"They're for little kids, Mag."

"I know, but I'd just like to go and watch. They all look like Shetlands."

Ruth knew she just wanted to think about Glory. "You go ahead. I want to find Mother and Daddy. Maybe they will give me money for some more cotton candy." She ran off, leaving Mag to work her way through the crowd to get near the fence encircling the pony ride.

The live ponies were hooked to a "turn" which forced them to go around and around. Mag didn't like it. It seemed so hard on the ponies to have to go around like that all day long.

The music began and the poor ponies started to move. Mag's heart almost stopped beating! "Glory! It's Glory!" Mag looked around for Ruth, but her friend hadn't returned. Glory, wearing a bright red plume, looked miserable. When she heard the familiar voice, she whinnied and tried to break free. The small boy on her back was frightened and promptly hit her with the reins.

Mag edged closer to the fence. When Glory came around again, she whispered: "Glory, what are you doing here?" The pony whinnied again but was forced to go on around.

Mag ran around the fence, talking to the pony the whole time. The manager of the pony rides saw Mag. "Get away from here, kid, right now. Git!"

Mag looked at the surly man. "I just want to talk with that Shetland. She used to be mine—or at least she used to live on our farm." Mag's heart was throbbing; she had never felt so helpless in her life.

"Well, she ain't yours no more. Now git away from here and stop bothering her."

Mag backed away from the fence without taking her green eyes off Glory, who kept trying to break free. Harnessed securely to the sturdy rigging, the horse whinnied. The boy on her back was now kicking her. Mag looked into the pony's face and saw the tears rolling down.

Her own eyes filled with tears of hurt and anger as she ran back, unmindful of the consequences, and hollered at the child astride Glory, "You stop hitting that pony, and I mean it."

"You shut up," the boy responded curtly. "My mother paid for me to ride this horse, and I'll hit him if I want to."

Mag tried to speak kindly in an effort to stop the boy from mistreating Glory. "You're not supposed to *hurt* the pony."

But the turn kept moving, and the boy was soon gone. Mag stood back a bit, aware that the manager might return. She was almost frantic.

Her own eyes filled with tears of hurt and anger as she ran back, unmindful of the consequences, and hollered at the child astride Glory, "You stop hitting that pony, and I mean it."

"You shut up," the boy responded curtly. "My mother paid for me to ride this horse, and I'll hit him if I want to."

Mag tried to speak kindly in an effort to stop the boy from mistreating Glory. "You're not supposed to *hurt* the pony."

Sure enough, the man walked beside Glory and began snapping his whip across her nose to settle her down. Mag winced with each blow. Her tears were flowing freely now.

The man finally stopped the merry-go-round and helped the riders off. He glared at Mag. She glared back at him through her tears.

More children were being put on the ponies. Still Glory tried to get free. She kept rearing up, so that the man couldn't get a little girl to mount her. He went on to the next pony. When they all had riders, he went back to Glory and again hit her across the face. "Now you do right, Sheltie, or I'll unharness you and beat the daylights out of you like I did this morning."

Mag was desperately trying to think of a way to help the little Shetland when she heard her father's voice. "Mag, come here."

She turned and ran to him. Through her tears, she told the story to her father. Bystanders were looking and listening.

"But, Mag, the carnival owns the pony now. We can't interfere," Mr. Henderson explained.

Glory was still struggling and jarring the whole apparatus. The man was trying to get her under control. Now all the ponies were trying to break harness. The honey-colored Shetland had them all nervous and uncomfortable.

The operator yelled at Mag, "Now, you see what you've done, you brat! You got the whole shebang out of kilter. Git from here before I call the law."

Mr. Henderson put his arm around Mag's shoulder and spoke to the operator. "I think you should understand the situation. My daughter here had this pony on our place all summer and grew quite attached to her...."

The man interrupted. "Well, why in blazes didn't you let her keep her there? This pony's nothing but a troublemaker for me." He pulled out a grimy handkerchief and mopped his bald head.

Mr. Henderson blurted out: "Well, why don't you ask your boss if he'll sell this troublemaker to me?"

Mag wiped her eyes on her sleeve and looked quickly up at her father. She couldn't believe it. Mrs. Henderson walked over and squeezed her daughter's shoulders.

The operator scratched his stubbled chin. "I'll ask him. You leave your name and address with me, and I'll get him to contact you. I sure ain't got no use for the ornery thing."

Mr. Henderson gave the man his name and address and walked back to his family. He looked first at Mag and then at his smiling wife. "I just couldn't stand to see her so miserable. We'll work something out."

Mag grabbed her daddy around his waist and hugged with all her might. He wasn't like King Henry at all. She also knew it took a lot for him to give in. "Daddy, I know I'm getting too big to ride her, but I love her so, and I *will* want a big horse later. I promise."

Her daddy hugged her and nodded. Mag went over to speak to Glory, while the operator unharnessed the now peaceful ponies for the night.

"You're coming home, Glory. Tomorrow!" There were no tears now on Glory's face nor on Mag's.

Ruth stepped up to her best friend. "I'm so happy for you, Mag." They held hands and walked to the truck together.

Little did they know that there were still many things in store for Glory.

CHAPTER TEN

Lost!

As they bumped along toward the carnival grounds in the old truck, Mag held tight to the bridle in her lap. Mr. Henderson smoked his pipe in silence, but his daughter wanted to talk.

"Daddy, I wish I could find a job. I would save my money to buy a saddle for Glory."

He smiled. "You're too young to get a job. Besides, by the time you save enough for a saddle, you'll be far too big for Glory. Now, be reasonable. You love the little pony: for that reason and *only* for that reason, we're going to buy her from the carnival people. But you must understand that farm folks who work hard for their living can't afford to have useless animals on their place."

Mr. Hendersons's pipe had gone out, and he searched his pocket for a match. Mag listened respectfully. She was so grateful to be getting Glory back that she dared not say too much. She spoke in her softest voice, "Mother says people need some things in their lives that aren't useful, like flowers, because they help to make a hard life more bearable."

"And your mother is right, but this winter Glory will need feed bought from the store or she'll eat the corn we raised for the hogs and chickens, and she can do nothing in return for her keep. We have a good life, Mag, but only because we are careful with our money and don't mind hard work.''

Mag thought about her father's remarks as they drove along. Then the girl had an idea. ''Say, you know how the carnival man had Glory harnessed to that rig?'' she asked. ''Well, why couldn't she be trained to pull a plow? She could plow the garden and Mother's flower beds and little patches. I could teach her to do it. She's quite young, you know. Then she would be earning her keep.'' She waited for her father to consider her idea.

''She might be able to do that,'' Pa said thoughtfully.

Mag continued, ''She's half Welsh, and Welsh ponies are known for their strength. I read that the ponies in Wales pull heavy coal wagons.''

Mr. Henderson smiled big. ''You've been doing some research, haven't you, Mag?''

She smiled and hoped.

They were nearing the carnival grounds. ''What the...'' Mr. Henderson brought the old truck to a halt.

Mag's eyes grew wide. The carnival ground was clean. Not a tent remained, not a trailer, not a cotton candy stand, not a single pony.

''They're gone, Mag. Moved on.''

''But, Daddy, they said they'd let you know.'' She felt sick to her stomach.

''Well, they often stay just one night. I guess the head man didn't want to sell her—or maybe the operator didn't talk with him.'' Mr. Henderson shook his head. It had been a trip for nothing.

Mag squeezed the bridle. ''What'll we do, Daddy? Can we go and find the carnival? Please?'' The girl was almost in tears again. ''We just have to find her, Daddy.''

Mr. Henderson heaved a deep sigh and turned the truck toward the little town and the constable's office.

The constable was out of his office, but a man standing on the street told them that the carnival had left before daylight for Medley. Mr. Henderson thanked him and walked back to the truck where Mag waited, still clutching Glory's bridle.

"It's just twelve miles over there. We'll go and see, I guess."

Mag's hopes soared again.

"Small carnivals like this usually travel by truck. The big ones go by train." Mr. Henderson was making conversation for her benefit.

"Yes, sir." She stared at the neat patch in her blue jeans and wondered why things were happening as they were.

It seemed a long twelve miles to Mag, but finally they came to the little village of Medley snuggled in the mountains. It wasn't hard to find the carnival. Bright posters announcing its coming were everywhere.

Mag and her father began looking for the pony rides. "There, Daddy, over there."

The same knotty little man with the whip was getting his rig ready.

"Daddy, I don't see Glory. She's not with the others."

Their voices jerked the operator to attention. "You lookin' for that trouble makin' Shetland, are you? She got away. Tore down the corral and took two of my best ponies with her." He spat tobacco juice to one side. "You gonna pay for 'em?"

Mr. Henderson was aggravated. "Well, I'll be darned."

Mag looked up at her father. A tightness filled her chest. "Now, she's lost. Let's go look for her."

The carnival man was waiting for an answer. "You gonna pay for them ponies or not? It was that stubborn filly that led 'em away."

Mr. Henderson looked the man in the eye. "No, I'm not going to pay for them. It wasn't my responsibility. If they are found, I'll have the constable run them through the auction sale and send you what they bring."

The carnival man wiped his chin with the back of his hand. "Well, I guess that'll have to do, but if that hightailed little filly hadn't led them..."

Mr. Henderson interrupted: "Maybe, but then maybe if *you* were kinder to the animals, they wouldn't want to run away." With that, he took Mag's hand, and they headed for the truck.

The operator yelled after them, "You sayin' I ain't good to these ponies? That's all you know...." He was still ranting and raving as they left the carnival grounds.

When they reached the truck, Mag looked at its wooden side planks. They had worked a good hour putting them on so Glory could ride home in the truck. Now, what use had it been? Mag felt heartsick. "Can't we ride over the countryside and look for them, Daddy?"

Mr. Henderson was firm. "Now, Mag, I've spent the best part of a day trying to get Glory. We have to get back to the farm. I'll alert all the farmers around to keep an eye out for the ponies. That's the best I can do."

Mag leaned back and tried to think. "What a mess. I can't imagine Glory leading those ponies away. Maybe she followed one of them."

"I suspect she had a lot to do with their escape," Mr. Henderson replied. "You know how high-spirited she is, and she is the leader type."

In spite of her worry, Mag smiled to herself. Just imagine, three Shetlands escaping and going to heaven-only-knows-where like fugitives. She was sure they were having a great time being free and not having to go around and around all day long. Then the girl grew sober, wondering if she'd ever see the little pony again.

A few miles away, three Shetlands, two shaggy and one sleek because she was half Welsh, were eating corn in a field they had broken into. From nowhere, a shot rang out and then another one. A farmer yelled and fired again. The sleek pony led the others to safety outside the field. She turned her head in all directions, trying to get her bearings. Her intentions were to find a big white house where there was a sun-tanned little girl.

The lead pony whinnied loudly as they trotted down the road, leaving a cloud of dust on that hot, summer day.

CHAPTER ELEVEN

The Ice Cream Party

Mag and her mother were in the kitchen canning peas. "Mag, it looks like this will be the last of the peas this summer. With the weather so dry, no more blooms will come to give us peas."

Mag added a teaspoon of salt to each quart jar of peas before her mother put on the lids. "I'm tired of fooling with them anyway," she said.

Mrs. Henderson knew Mag wasn't herself lately. If only she could do something to take the girl's mind off the lost pony.

Mag wiped the jars with a clean cloth, and Mrs. Henderson tightened the lids. She had never seen her daughter so sad in her life.

"Mag, doesn't some homemade ice cream sound good? We could add some peaches to make it even better. And you could ask Ruth and her family over if you like."

Mag smiled. She knew her mother was trying to get her mind off Glory. "I'd like that, Mother. It's so hot today. Ice cream ought to be *really* good."

"Fine. I'll send your daddy into town to get some ice, and we'll have an ice cream party. You've worked hard today helping me."

She hugged her daughter close, and Mag put her arms around her. "Mother, will I ever see poor, little Glory again?"

She stroked Mag's hair. "Sure you will, honey." Mrs. Henderson hoped she was right.

It was such fun making ice cream. Everyone gathered under the giant oak in the front yard and took turns at the crank. When the children could no longer turn it and the grownups had to take over, everyone knew it wouldn't be long until it was ready to eat.

It took two gallons to satisfy everyone. The party turned into an afternoon affair. The white-headed Johnson children were having a good time playing chase, while Ruth and Mag stood to one side and talked. Meanwhile, the adults discussed the crops, the weather and other things that adults usually talk about.

Under the big tree, Mr. Henderson and Mr. Johnson finished their ice cream and leaned back in their straight chairs. A steady breeze began to blow and a few leaves fell to the ground. The men looked at the sky.

"Looks like we might get some rain out of this," Mr. Henderson remarked.

Mr. Johnson spoke, "Looks funny over that way, kind of stormy."

A flash of lightning far off moved in closer, and thunder rumbled through the mountains repeatedly. The wind began to blow harder, but it felt good to Mag and Ruth.

"They're the cutest things in the world," Ruth commented about the Hendersons' new baby pigs.

"A baby horse is pretty, too. I believe they are called foals."

"Yeah, foals." Ruth knew at once that Mag was thinking of Glory, so she hurried to change the subject. "Here it is August! School will be starting soon."

"I wonder if there'll be any new kids there." Mag liked the way the strong breeze blew through her long hair.

"There never are. Guess we'll have to look at the same old faces."

They both laughed as they watched the sky. It had turned a peculiar color.

Mrs. Johnson gathered her children into their old truck. Mr. Johnson turned to Mag's father. "See you, Henry. We best get home. Martha has clothes on the line, and I have to see to the stock."

Mrs. Johnson thanked Mrs. Henderson for the enjoyable afternoon as everyone else said their goodbyes.

Mrs. Henderson turned to Mag. "Let's go into the house."

The giant oak heaved and groaned as it blew with the wind. A dead branch fell to the ground and leaves scattered.

Mr. Henderson spoke with authority, "This could be serious. I'll see to the cattle, Mother. You and Mag best get some bedding; we'll go to the storm cellar."

Everyone in the hills had a cellar for storing canned foods, fruit, turnips and such. It was a good place to get out of a storm, too.

"All right, Daddy," Mrs. Henderson agreed. "Be sure to see that my banty hen and her chicks are safe in their coop. Mag, you get the bed rolls and I'll gather a little something to eat. This may last several hours, and I've never seen a time when you and your daddy weren't hungry." She patted Mag on the head and went to the kitchen.

Mag glanced out the window on her way to the closet and saw the chickens running toward the chicken house. Their feathers were blowing backwards, making them look funny. The wind was blowing so hard, the trees seemed to be bowing . "Oh, Glory, I hope you're not out in this," she said aloud.

Lady, the collie dog, hurried down the steps to enter the cellar. Mag patted her. "You're afraid of this storm, aren't you, girl?"

Mr. Henderson stepped aside to let the collie enter. Lady went to a corner and lay down.

The rain came down in sheets, but Mag and her family were safe and dry in the cellar while the wind ripped and howled above them.

Mag enjoyed the cellar. It was cool and dimly lit by a single kerosene lantern. She loved the good smell of the earth and the cool air.

Mrs. Henderson and Mag had placed many jars of foodstuffs there. They stored carrots, turnips, rhubarb and potatoes in boxes. A basket of apples, too, had been carefully wrapped and stored in the coolness of the cellar.

Mag looked at the apples and thought of how Glory enjoyed them. Her throat tightened. She tried to turn her thoughts to other things to keep from crying.

Meanwhile, inside a cave, high in the mountains, three Shetlands, one of them half Welsh, stood safe and dry, watching the storm. There were cuts on their legs and across their faces. Two of the ponies stood to one side, looking to their leader, the sleek one, who eyed the storm and nickered softly to them.

Much later, the Hendersons came up from the cellar and surveyed the land. The wind had done some damage but nothing so severe that a hammer and some nails couldn't repair it. A section of the tin roof had blown off the barn, and some tar paper had torn loose from the chicken house and truck shed. Limbs and leaves carpeted the wet ground and one of the wash tubs had blown clear across the fence.

They would get up early the next morning and repair things. It had been quite an afternoon, and everyone was ready for bed.

CHAPTER TWELVE

The Search

The next morning it was still too wet to do much. Mrs. Henderson let Mag and Lady go for a walk. She told Mag she was not to go too far and get lost.

Of course, Mag would not dispute her mother's word, but she didn't think she could ever get lost in these hills. They were so familiar to her; she and Glory had covered nearly every square foot of them, or so she thought.

Mag packed several apples, some cookies and a fruit jar filled with cold water into a pouch with a shoulder strap. The pouch, made by her mother, was yellow with pretty embroidered flowers. It was one of Mag's prize possessions.

"Now, Mag, I'll expect you back before too long," her mother reminded her. "You can look at the sun and guess the time. And watch out for copperheads. They're plentiful this time of year."

Mag smiled. "I'll be careful, and I won't be gone long." She kissed her mother and whistled to Lady. Then they were off.

Mrs. Henderson knew that Mag would be looking for Glory. Someone said they had seen several small horses in the vicinity, and Mag just had to go and look. Mrs. Henderson was not too worried about the girl, especially since the moonshiners had confessed their crime and were safely behind bars.

Mrs. Henderson smiled to herself as she recalled the constable standing on the front porch watching Mag and Ruth jumping and clapping when he told them the moonshiners had been jailed. They had congratulated the constable and invited him to sit down to enjoy some fresh chocolate cake and milk. "So, there went my dessert," Mrs. Henderson mused, "but it was certainly for a worthy cause."

Now Mag was drinking in the beauty of the Ozark Mountains. "Ah, Lady, look, the first goldenrods." They got her pondering about school, since the yellow bushes always were in bloom when classes began.

Lady was sniffing rabbit tracks. The dog knew she couldn't catch anything but was enjoying the activity. She was old now and it was time to take it easy. The Hendersons would feed her even if she never caught another rabbit.

Mag looked up at the late summer sky and saw buzzards circling smoothly overhead in search of food. It gave her an uneasy feeling.

She looked over her shoulder. She could still see the top of the farmhouse through the woods. The mountains were high enough here to be interesting and beautiful, but she had never been much farther than this alone.

Mag wanted to climb to the highest peak and scan the horizon for signs of the three lost ponies. She calculated her directions. First, she looked again toward the farmhouse far below and then up at the top of the nearest hill. "Surely, Lady, I can find my way back from that little old hill. What do you think?"

The collie responded with a whine. She was tired already.

"Well, I'm just going *straight* to the top of that hill. I'll look and come back. It's only a hundred yards or so. How can I possibly lose my way doing that?"

Lady was panting heavily now. She wanted only to go back to her cool place under the porch.

"Well, you just wait here for me. Here, I'll even leave my shoulder bag with you. You just rest, and I'll be back in a jiffy." Mag reached down and put the strap around Lady's neck and then giggled at how silly the old dog looked. Lady whined.

"Now, stay," the girl commanded. Then she continued up the mountain.

Mag had often been hiking in the mountains with her parents, but they had come in the wintertime when the chores were over and done and the copperhead snakes had gone into hiding for the winter. Mag fondly remembered that Lady had often come with the family. Following the trail with Mag, she had picked up a rabbit's scent in the snow and had chased the smaller animal for the longest time. Her short yelps had echoed over the snowclad mountains.

Now the August sun was hot, and Mag was drenched in her own perspiration. She was enjoying the mature feeling of hiking alone. Her intention had been to climb straight to the top of the mountain, but rocks too high to climb or crevices too deep to jump prevented her from going straight up. Soon, without realizing it, she was zigzagging toward the top.

Finally, she reached the top, very hot and out of breath. As she stood, she felt the wind blow against her. It cooled her. She sucked in her breath. The beautiful view was overwhelming.

"This has just got to be the most beautiful place in the whole wide world!" she cried. She wondered why her father hadn't built their home here so they could have this view. Of course, it wasn't practical for farming, but it *was* a terrific place to be. The puffy clouds seemed so close. With a feeling of utter happiness, Mag reached her arms toward the clouds and laughed aloud.

She looked down to her left, and her breath caught in her throat. She saw a Shetland pony grazing on a mountain ledge. It didn't seem far away at all. She put her hand to her mouth in surprise and strained to see better. Soon only a tail was visible. "Glory, Glory!" Mag yelled. Then even the tail was gone.

Excited that she might have found the pony, Mag started down the hill, completely forgetting her promise to go straight back to the spot where Lady waited. Raspberry briars tore at her clothing and face and caught her hair. She fell many times and felt her feet bleeding from the sharp rocks, but she kept going, calling the pony as she made her way down.

"Please nicker or whinny, Glory!" She stopped to listen, but a colony of crows were cawing noisily in a nearby hollow.

"For once, I wish they'd hush." And they did. She wondered why. Suddenly, a loud whinny echoed over the mountain. Goose bumps raced up the girl's arms to the top of her head.

"Glory!" she screamed as loud as she could. No pony or horse in the world had as loud a whinny as Glory.

Suddenly, Mag broke into an opening which at one time had been cleared for pasture. Standing on the other side of the field was Glory. Next to her was another Shetland with a shaggy coat.

"Glory!" Mag ran toward the pony as fast as she could. The shaggy pony turned and ran into the woods, but Glory, whinnying all the way, ran to meet Mag.

The girl fell on the pony's neck, hugged her as tightly as she could and cried with happiness and relief. Glory was trying to eat her hair and whinny at the same time.

Mag finally turned Glory loose and saw a shaggy pony standing behind a bush. "Hello, little pony." She walked slowly toward it. "Is this your friend, Glory? Where is the other one?"

Mag walked toward the shaggy pony. Then the other Shetland returned from the woods. There was an ugly wound in the pony's flank. Glory nickered quietly as though to say that the girl wouldn't harm them. The ponies quieted down.

Mag felt pity for the poor animals. "Looks like some vicious dogs have been at you. You poor things." She looked at the Shetland limping out from behind the bush. It too was hurt. Mag walked up and gently inspected the pony's hoof. A rock was deeply embedded in it. Try as she might, Mag couldn't get the rock out. She eased the leg down and stood with her hands on her hips. "Well, Glory, you have a couple of crippled friends. No wonder you wouldn't leave them." There were ugly scratches on Glory, too.

For the first time, Mag felt fear. The excitement of finding Glory had made her forget all the things she was supposed to remember. She looked at the sun and knew it was a long time past lunch. She began to worry. "We're in a real mess, Glory, a real mess."

"Hello there."

With her heart in her throat, Mag whirled around. She found herself looking into the face of a boy a few years older than she. "Hi," she answered.

He was tall, with a shock of black hair and the bluest eyes Mag had ever seen. He wore cut-off jeans and a white tee shirt and was barefoot. In his right hand he carried a shotgun. "Them your ponies?"

"Yes and no. You see, I'm in a real mess."

"What kind?" He was friendly and seemed interested.

She told him of her plight and then heaved a sigh. "Sounds like a made-up story, doesn't it?"

The boy smiled. "Well, it does sound a little far-fetched, but I have no reason to doubt you." He shook his head. "Runaway ponies from a carnival."

For the first time, Mag felt fear. The excitement of finding Glory had made her forget all the things she was supposed to remember. She looked at the sun and knew it was a long time past lunch. She began to worry. "We're in a real mess, Glory, a real mess."

"Yes, and the worst part about it is that we'll never find our way back over the mountain, and I don't want to leave these injured ponies here."

She had completely forgotten her manners. "Oh, I'm Mag Henderson. I live somewhere over that mountain." She pointed.

"I'm Warren Stephenson, and I live on this farm. You're a long way from home."

Mag nodded as the Stephenson boy walked over to the ponies, talking softly.

Mag told him about the stone in the pony's hoof. He pulled out a pocket knife and deftly removed it. The pony was able to walk without limping. Mag smiled.

He took one pony by each halter. "Get your pony, and let's lead them slowly to our barn. It isn't too far up that hollow."

He sounded confident, and Mag felt he would take care of everything. She took Glory's halter and followed the tall, dark-headed boy.

"Here, let me lead one of the ponies so you can carry your gun," she said.

"Thanks. I bring this along when I come looking for a stray cow or horse, so many wolves and mountain lions up here."

Mag shivered, wondering how near she had been to them.

"We'll put the ponies in the barn, and I'll get my dad to drive you home. If you left early this morning, your folks will be worried."

Mag swallowed hard. But the consolation that she had found her pony would make it easier to face her worried parents. She looked down at the scratches on her feet and legs and suddenly realized she had had neither food nor water since early morning. She was thirsty and very hungry and would be glad to get home.

Later, Mag sat on the bed in her room and ran her finger

over and over the dutch doll in the patchwork quilt. Her parents stood together like an iron fortress watching her. She knew she was in trouble. At least they hadn't said much in front of the Stephenson boy and his father.

Mr. Henderson spoke. "Magdalen, you've done a very serious wrong."

She kept staring at the doll in the quilt.

"You've worried us a great deal by going over the mountain alone without permission. You disobeyed your mother. When Lady came back with your shoulder pouch, your mother went in search of you. She was frantic that a mountain lion with cubs or a pack of wolves had attacked you." Mr. Henderson's voice was sad but very strong and deep.

Mag felt so ashamed. Then her mother spoke: "You greatly frightened us. You are never to do this again, Mag."

Mag looked up quickly. "I was so excited about Glory that I wasn't thinking straight."

Neither of her parents spoke, but Mag had already learned her lesson. She *would* remember to listen to her parents the next time, lost pony or not.

CHAPTER THIRTEEN

Glory Proves
Her Worth

The runaway ponies were treated by the veterinarian and, just as Mr. Henderson said, sold at the auction. The money for them and Glory was sent to the carnival owner. Mag was thrilled. Now Glory *was* her pony.

"Mother, it's just wonderful that so many good things are happening, isn't it?" She danced around the room in delight. It was a beautiful day, and a breeze was blowing. Best of all, Grandfather Henderson was coming for a visit!

Mrs. Henderson held one end of a feather pillow under her chin and pulled on a fresh pillow case. Then she puffed it until it resembled a white cloud. "Yes, Mag, it is very nice. But remember, if good things happened all the time, we wouldn't be nearly as happy about them, would we?"

Mag dusted the bed posts. "I guess not. If we smelled roses all the time, we'd get sick of 'em, I expect."

Mrs. Henderson nodded and smiled. "I expect so."

Mag swung around and looked at herself in the floor-length mirror. The mirror was very old. It made her look wiggly. She giggled. "Does Grandfather Henderson like living with Aunt Clarissy now that Grandmother is dead?"

"I hope so dear. Aunt Clarissy is a caring daughter. Your daddy thinks very highly of his sister."

Mag dusted the wiggly mirror and watched herself as she talked. "She's an old maid, isn't she?"

"Well, dear, I believe they are properly called spinsters. But your Aunt Clarissy has a full and happy life."

"I bet so. She reminds me of a ball bouncing around." Mag smiled as she thought about her aunt. She was short and lively with salt and pepper hair and dark-rimmed glasses.

Mrs. Henderson laughed aloud. "Yes, she does and *we'd* best bounce downstairs and see about supper. Your father and grandfather will be here soon."

For no special reason, Mag hugged her mother and skipped downstairs.

Her mother called after her. "You're like a bouncing ball yourself, young lady." She smiled after her daughter.

Grandfather Henderson was tall and slim with hair whiter than any snow Mag had ever seen. His eyes were like bright shiny marbles. He laughed easily and talked about Grandmother as though she were still alive and with him. "Henry, I believe Mag looks more like your mother every time I see her." Mag smiled.

Mr. Henderson looked her way. "Well, some, but I guess you can see it more than we can."

Mag sat on the arm of her grandfather's chair. "Granddaddy, will you go with me and Glory to explore the river if it's nice weather?"

He patted her leg. "Well, honey, I don't know why not if your mother says it's okay."

Mrs. Henderson smiled at him. "She may go if you promise not to go too far. The river can be dangerous at certain points where it's wide and rushing."

"We'll do just as you say." He winked up at Mag. Mag nodded in agreement.

Grandfather Henderson walked slowly along the beach puffing his pipe. Mag followed astride Glory. She could imagine that one day her father would look just like him.

"Mag, you're a very fortunate young lady." She was glad he hadn't called her a little girl, even if that's what she was to most grown-ups. "You live in a part of God's world that is absolutely beautiful." He waved his thin arms to take in everything. "These Ozark Mountains, this river, the rich, fertile valleys always refresh me so."

"Don't they have these things in Virginia?"

"Oh, yes, certainly, but I live in the flat part of Virginia. It has its own special beauty, too."

"I know. Our teacher said that even hot deserts are beautiful, especially early morning when everything is fresh."

The old man nodded. "True. Everywhere beauty abounds. You just have to open your eyes wide and look for it sometimes." He stopped to light his pipe again. "Just what did you want to explore along this beautiful river? Anything in particular?"

Mag shrugged her slight shoulders. "I'd like to see if we can find a beaver den. But what I really and truly would love to do is to explore some of the caves around here. There are plenty of them." She reached over and patted Glory's neck. The pony's response was her usual soft nicker.

Grandfather chuckled. "Well, we aren't prepared for that. One needs ropes, lanterns, picks and special footwear; and a lot more knowledge of caves than your old Granddaddy has."

Mag grinned. "I know, but when I get older, I want to study all about caves. Then I'll know how to explore them and which interesting things to look for."

"That's wise thinking, Mag. Say, do you know what people who study and explore caves are called?"

"No, sir."

"They are called spelunkers."

Mag giggled. "That's a funny name."

"Yes, but a very serious profession."

Mag hoped she wouldn't forget the name.

Grandfather stopped and looked long at the river trickling over pebbles and rocks. "With any luck, we ought to find a beaver den along this river. Have you seen any signs?"

"No, but my friend Ruth's brother saw some signs up-river: trees gnawed down and a little slide where they had been getting into the river."

The old man put his hands into his pockets. "Well, those are good signs all right. We'll go on up a bit farther."

Glory nibbled at grass near the river trail. Mag slid off her back and carried the lunch bag over her shoulder. "I heard, Granddaddy, that a beaver is a natural builder and does a lot for the land."

"That's right, Maggie. They're the best of engineers. The dams they build make ponds that fill with water in rainy seasons. Then, during dry weather, the dams give out water slowly for the crops and stock. They help mankind a lot." The old man continued to eye the banks and wet sand for tracks. "When I was a boy, we trapped beaver; their furs brought a lot of money even then. When they almost became extinct, the government passed a law to protect them. That was good. Someday, beavers'll be plentiful again."

Mag couldn't bear to think of hurting a beaver, or any other animal for that matter. She did take a switch to Glory once in a while but mostly to scare her. "I'd never trap anything," she said.

"Yet, you would have long ago. That was one of the main ways of making a living. In fact, that's the reason this great country was settled: the fur trappers kept going farther west, looking for good trapping. They opened up new country." The older Mr. Henderson ran a hand through his thick white hair and thought back over the years. "Good and bad came of it, though," he admitted. "Some of the traders had no conscience. They killed animals for no reason and did a lot of harm to the Indians. After all, the prairies were their *home.*" He paused with a sigh.

Mag didn't want to talk about it anymore. It saddened her. She pointed ahead to a clump of deep yellow flowers. They were a kind that she had never seen before. A heavy, sweet scent filled the air. "What are they, Granddaddy?"

"Don't know, lassie, but they sure smell good. On the way back, you should pick a few for your mother. I always did that for your grandmother, and she was so happy over them."

Mag wished she could remember her grandmother. Suddenly, though, she was distracted from her thoughts. She spied several trees marked by an unmistakable sign. The trees had been gnawed down by beavers. She ran ahead, shouting, "Look, Granddaddy!"

Glory followed slowly, eating all the while.

Grandfather Henderson stepped over several boulders to take a closer look. "Beavers did this work all right. I'll just bet there's a whole colony of them."

Mag inspected the trees. "They look like they've been put in a giant pencil sharpener. But why do they just cut the trees down and leave them?"

"Oh, they'll come back at night to drag them below the water. I understand they can build houses sturdier than we can, even with all our tools."

"Gosh, look there! That's a beaver slide sure as the world."
Mag scrambled down the bank of the river to get a better look.

"You won't likely see a beaver now. They come out at night
mostly."

"I know. But just look at the cute little slide. I can just see
them lining up to slide down into the water. What fun they must
have."

Grandfather chuckled at the girl's lively imagination.

Neither of them knew that at that very moment a beaver was
under the water just feet away from Mag. He was waiting for the
pair to leave so he could go on with his work and play. Beavers
can stay underwater for up to fifteen minutes, but his fifteen
minutes' worth of air was almost all used up! A rodent-looking
head eased up out of the water behind a log. Only Glory saw it.
She whinnied loudly, but instantly the beaver melted back into
the water.

Mag looked around at Glory, whose head was bobbing up
and down. "I wish I could understand you." The pony wished it
too.

"Mag, your pony's smart, but you mustn't ever let her get
the upper hand on you."

"No, sir, I won't." Of course, Glory felt the same way. She
wasn't about to let Mag get an upper hand on her.

Mag and her grandfather turned back to the slide and the
felled trees. It made Mag's jaws ache just to think about cutting
down a tree with one's teeth.

Grandfather sat on a low boulder. "You know, those beavers
really have quite a society. When a mother beaver is killed or
dies, another mother will take the babies and raise them as her
own. Every beaver in a colony feels a responsibility for the young
ones."

A lump came in Mag's throat. That was one of the sweetest things she had ever heard.

Grandfather looked up as a large, colorful bird flew overhead. "Well, that's the first pileated woodpecker I've seen since I was a boy. That bird nearly became extinct, too."

Mag watched the brilliant black, red and white bird settle in a nearby tree. "Oh, there's lots of them; just a big old woodpecker."

"Just a big old woodpecker," Grandfather mimicked, "but one that might be extinct someday."

Mag hadn't realized that. It made her glad that the bird was there.

"Missy, why don't you hunt up a nice place to eat that good lunch your mother fixed for us."

Mag hopped over the rocks. "You getting tired, Granddaddy?"

The white-haired man smiled. "Well, I'm more tired than you are, Maggie, and you know your mother will be worried if we're gone too long."

"You're right. Let's go back to the spot by the pretty yellow flowers. That okay?" She reached down and got Glory's reins.

"Sounds fine, just let me..." his voice trailed off.

Mag jerked around, her heart beating wildly. Behind her, Grandfather had stumbled and fallen backward on the rocks. She ran to his side. "Granddaddy, you all right?"

He was very still. She lifted his head and found blood in his white hair and on his face.

Mag was nearly paralyzed with fear. He began to stir and fear changed to hope. "Open your eyes, Grandfather! Please!"

His eyelids quivered. In a very weak voice, he mumbled, "Sorry, Maggie, don't know what happened. Just blacked out for

Mag was nearly paralyzed with fear. He began to stir and fear changed to hope. "Open your eyes, Grandfather! Please!"

a minute. I'll be all right." He put his hand on his head and felt the blood. "Had a nasty fall, didn't I?"

"Yes, you did, Granddaddy." She was close to tears.

He tried to sit up, but instantly lay back on the pebbly beach. "You best go for help, lassie. I feel too weak to walk."

Mag couldn't leave him there alone. It was at least a mile back to the house.

"Glory! You can ride Glory, Granddaddy. She'll get you home, and everything will be fine."

The old man glanced at the pony, whose ears perked up. "I don't know. Maybe."

"Sure you can. I'll help you stand and get on her. Why, with your long legs, you can just about step over her. I'll lead her nice and easy."

"Looks like you're running the show. Call her over here, lassie."

"Come here, Glory." The pony obeyed without coaxing.

It didn't take long to help her grandfather mount. He held his toes up so they wouldn't drag on the ground. Mag put their lunch bag around her shoulder and led Glory slowly and gently, telling the pony all the while not to be rough; that her grandfather was ill. The old man, weak and tired, leaned forward in a slumping position.

Certainly, Glory wasn't going to be rough. She knew the old man was sick. Carefully she picked her way among the rocks. Mag kept looking at Grandfather. It seemed an eternity before they walked into the front yard. Mag began yelling for her mother to come quickly.

After the doctor had gone, Mag sat in a chair by her grandfather's bed. Mr. and Mrs. Henderson stood together at the foot.

"Well, Maggie, he said it was my heart giving me a little fit. Now I'll have to be careful like an old man should." In spite of his condition, her grandfather could still chuckle.

Mr. Henderson looked at his father sternly but with love. "No more hiking on the river for you, Pop."

"No more for a while, son, but I want to tell you something about that little Shetland. If she had been six inches taller, I couldn't have gotten on her even with Mag's help. I've never seen a smarter animal. She was as gentle as a rocking chair, and that's a fact."

Mag squeezed her grandfather's hand. She was grateful he was going to be all right and happy he had spoken so well about Glory. "I'd better go tell her you're all right."

The adults smiled at one another, but, as a matter of fact, the little Shetland-Welsh pony was still waiting by the fence. She seemed glad when Mag came running over with the news.

CHAPTER FOURTEEN

A Pony Needs Discipline

Sweat ran down Mag's sun-browned face. She was determined to make a decent riding and plow pony out of Glory. "You have to obey, Glory. This bit in your mouth says you will do as I say or else."

Glory was as stubborn as her young trainer and just as determined to do as *she* pleased. It was a tug of war. Today Glory did not want to be ridden. She had thrown Mag a half-dozen times already.

Finally, Mr. Henderson came into the pasture. "Mag, do you remember when you disobeyed and your mother had to punish you?"

Mag squinted under the bright sun. "Yes, sir."

"Well, she still loves you. Right?"

Mag was certain of that. She nodded.

"Well, my girl, you are going to have to punish Glory, too, and make her mind you."

"But, Daddy, she doesn't understand. Besides, I already switched her, and it didn't do a frazzlin' bit of good."

Mr. Henderson studied the Shetland filly. Glory wished Mag's father would just go on back to the house. She had a feeling things weren't going to be as good as they had been.

"But, baby," Mr. Henderson explained, "you switch her one time and then the next time you let her get away with murder. That won't work."

Mag gave her father a prize-winning smile. "That's what you and Mother do with me."

He grinned. "Yes, and you see how undisciplined *you* are."

He tugged gently at one of her pigtails and went on. "You remember the Stephenson boy who found you? Well, his father tells me he's a natural horse trainer. I think I'll ask him about training Glory to the harness."

Mag's eyes widened. "Will he beat her?"

"No, of course not. He will have to punish her some, but I'm sure he'll only do the necessary. Glory's pretty smart; she will probably learn quickly what he wants her to do."

Mag was still concerned.

"You see, Mag, you love her so much and, well, she knows it and takes advantage of you. The Stephenson boy won't put up with her foolishness. She'll know that, too."

"I see. Gosh, it would be nice to have her mind and do what I want her to." She thought of the boy with the blue eyes. He did seem to know a lot about horses. It was easy to see that he loved them, too.

"Yes, Daddy, I think that would be good. How long will it take?"

"Well, smart as she seems, no more than three weeks... probably not that long."

"Could I see her?"

Mr. Henderson frowned. "Be better if you didn't. It would just make the training take longer."

"Seems she's been away from me more than she's been with me."

Mr. Henderson put his hand on her shoulder. "Well, she's got to be trained so she can earn her keep—or she has to go. Remember?"

Indeed she did remember. She sighed, "All right, Daddy."

He smiled and patted Glory on the rump, something Mag never dreamed she'd see. "Yes, little Shetland, with your intelligence, you might make a good horse for plowing the garden next spring."

Mag brightened. "Say, Daddy, I'm glad you're not like that mean old King of England, Henry VIII."

"What's this?"

"Oh, I'll have to tell you all about him sometime."

"Tell me now, baby."

"Okay."

Father and daughter walked arm in arm back toward the house as Mag told him what she had learned from the peddler.

Glory watched them and wondered what was in store for her. Whatever it was, she had no intentions of cooperating.

———————

Mag and Ruth finished their swim in the river and crawled up on the warm boulders to dry their hair in the early September sun.

"Mag, you must be happy that Glory's coming home today, aren't you?"

"I sure am. I wonder if she'll remember me." Mag felt the tangles in her hair and frowned.

"Oh, sure she will. Horses have good memories...or is that elephants?"

They giggled and Mag said, "But she might have switched her love over to Warren. They say he's good with horses."

"Oh, I imagine she likes him, but she *loves* you."

Mag wondered if Warren had had to hit the pony very much. Remembering the way Glory used to cry, Mag started to feel sad.

Mag and Ruth shed their wet cut-off jeans and shirts and put on dry clothes. Then, from the kitchen, Mrs. Henderson remarked, "Here comes Warren with your pony, Mag."

Mag ran as if the house were on fire, almost knocking Ruth down in her haste to get outside. "Watch out, Mag!" Ruth squealed as she followed her friend outside. She had never seen *anybody* so crazy over a horse.

"Hi, Mag."

"Hello, Warren."

The boy was riding a big dun-colored mare and leading the pony. Glory looked the same as when she had left.

Mag walked up to Glory who at once nudged her neck and let out a loud whinny. "Is she an obedient pony now?" she asked as she stroked the pony's mane.

The tall boy pushed his cap back and scratched his dark head. "Well, I'm afraid I couldn't do as good a job as I would have liked."

Mag looked puzzled.

"Well, what I mean is she's different from any pony I ever handled."

"Different?" Mrs. Henderson had come out on the porch.

The boy removed his cap when he saw her. "Yes. She's so full-spirited. I'm afraid Mag has spoiled her."

Mag jerked her head in his direction. "Spoiled her?"

"Yes. You let her have her own way too much. That's the very worst thing you can do."

"Well, I guess I did," Mag admitted.

He continued, "I know you love her, but if you don't exert your will over hers, she'll never amount to very much."

Mrs. Henderson added, "You'd best listen to Warren, Mag."

The boy nodded. "Oh, I have her so she obeys commands, and I think she'll make a nice plow horse. I put her in harness several days in a row and she behaved pretty well." He shook his head. "But she still has a stubborn streak a mile wide."

"Well, I guess they are sort of like people." Mag pulled a burr from the pony's long white mane.

Ruth spoke her opinion, "Looks like you'd have more luck if she had a saddle instead of a folded quilt."

Warren agreed readily. "Oh, she would. She doesn't feel that she's under anyone's command if her back is free. I could have done more with her if I had had a small saddle."

If Warren only knew how Mag longed for a saddle!

Then Warren said, "But your daddy said he just wanted her broken in for the plow first, and I think she is. Why don't you ride her and see if she's better."

"All right." Happily Mag walked to the pony's side to mount. She was a little embarrassed at the awkward manner in which she crawled on Glory's back. Suddenly she stopped, wincing at the sight before her. Several long welts marked Glory's side and neck. Anger filled the girl. She glared at the boy. "You call yourself a horse trainer and do this to my pony?" Tears welled up in her eyes.

Ruth ran around, looked at the pony's side and gasped.

"Mag!" Mrs. Henderson objected to her manner.

"But, Mother, look what he did to her." She continued to glare at the boy. Her hands tightened into fists.

Warren was getting agitated. "Now, listen. There's a heck of a lot you don't know about horses. You spoiled her rotten. If she was ever going to learn, I *had* to hit her. I didn't *enjoy* doing it."

Ruth asked, "So hard?"

Mrs. Henderson walked to the pony and looked at the ugly marks. She tightened her lips and looked directly at Warren. "I'm afraid I have to agree with the girls. I can't see the need for such cruelty."

"Mrs. Henderson," he began in his defense, "I was not cruel to the pony. Here, I'll show you." He climbed down off his own horse and walked a few yards away. "Come here, Glory."

Immediately the pony went to him. He rubbed her nose.

Mag was not satisfied. "Sure, she's afraid you'll beat her if she doesn't come."

Warren argued, "That's the whole point. You start with fear, but then habit takes over. Can't you understand?"

It was plain they couldn't. Warren got back on his horse and put on his cap. "I'm sorry. Maybe if you talk with Mr. Henderson, he could explain it to you." With that, he left the yard.

Mag clenched her fists. "Oh, I hate him!"

Mrs. Henderson chided her, "Mag, hate is a very strong word. You might hate this thing he did, but not the person."

"Yes, Mother." She hugged Glory, who whinnied and then snorted. It was plain to see she was glad to be back with Mag.

Mag and Ruth took Glory to the barn and Mrs. Henderson looked up the road after Warren. "Maybe us tenderhearted folks just can't understand."

Later, after inspecting the welts on Glory, Mr. Henderson talked with his wife and daughter. "Now, look, you two," he began as he walked up and down the length of the front porch. "In order to train a horse to mind, one has to let the animal know who is in command."

"But, Daddy, I don't have to be beaten to obey."

Henry looked at his child and sighed. "No, because you are rational. You can be *talked* to. Glory can't."

"Oh, Daddy, but she can."

"Now, Mag, you know what I mean. Animals don't respond to reasons and words. The only way to train them is to keep them under your control." He was searching for words to make them understand. "A horse or pony or any animal will not obey unless trained. If they are not trained, they are no good on a farm or anywhere else."

Mag looked at her father but said nothing.

Mr. Henderson turned to his wife. "Look, Mother. Do you remember that little mule we had? Her name was Betsy. That was before Mag was born. When I broke her in, I almost had to beat her to death. Glory's welts are not nearly so bad as Betsy's were. And she turned out to be the best little plow mule on the place." He shoved his hands in his pockets.

Mrs. Henderson remembered. "Yes, and I was mad at you for a month."

He smiled. "I know you were. I hated to have to hit her so hard. But if I had not exerted my will over hers, she might have hurt *you,* and then I would have *really* gotten rough."

Mrs. Henderson had to agree.

Mag was still puzzled. "Are all ponies and mules that way, that you have to hurt them so?"

He nodded. "To a degree. Those that are more high-spirited, like Glory, have to be punished more. Others are easier to control." He stroked his daughter's hair. There was compassion in his lean face. "Mag, the welts will go away and Glory will be useful to us both as a plow horse *and* for you to ride until your feet drag on the ground."

She smiled at her father and touched the hand on her shoulder. "I know you're right, Daddy, but it just seemed so cruel." Then she fell silent. There was nothing more to be said.

That night as Mag crawled between the cool, clean sheets of her little bed, she felt bad about the awful things she had said to Warren. "When I see him, I'll tell him I'm sorry."

She listened to the night sounds: the crickets, frogs and whippoorwills. Then she heard the best sound of all: Glory's loud whinny. It was her "good night" to Mag. She answered in a whisper, "Good night, little Shetland."

Glory wished she could tell Mag that she was the same in spite of the training, that she hadn't changed and still planned to throw Mag off her back every once in a while—just so the girl would know that she was still her same old self.

CHAPTER FIFTEEN

Happy Cowgirl

Mag was so excited she could hardly get dressed. Grandfather Henderson had sent her a letter explaining that he would never forget what the little pony had done for him. He wanted to repay them in some way, so he had ordered the finest little saddle in all of Virginia. It was coming in *today*. Grandfather said that Mag could consider it an early birthday present.

Mag tugged at the tangles in her hair. Birthday present, indeed! It was too *big* for a present, but she didn't care what he called it. Mag was too thrilled for words. She hurried even more when her daddy blew the horn to rush her.

Mag loved the combined general store and post office. There was everything from plow handles to bubble gum, and the store smelled of soap, candy, oranges and kerosene. She looked at the school supplies: She would be buying those next week. She opened a big jar of paste. The smell reminded her of when she was in the lower grades. She ran her hand over the thick tablets of Indian Chief paper and smelled the new cedar pencils.

Mr. Henderson finished talking with Mr. Johnson and then called to Mag to come to the back of the store. She skipped toward them. There before her very eyes was the prettiest and brightest saddle Mag had ever seen—not that she had seen very many, but she knew that this one was close to being perfect.

113

She whispered a soft "oh" and touched the rich, smooth leather. A happy feeling went through her. "It's just beautiful, Daddy."

The storekeeper said, "You take care of it, little lady, and it'll outlast the pony."

Mag certainly hoped not! But she smiled anyway, and said she surely would. Mag carried the saddle to the truck, even though Mr. Henderson had offered. Her happiness was almost more than she could bear.

"Stand still, Glory." Mag was getting hotter and madder by the minute. Glory kept sidestepping to keep her from putting the bright saddle blanket across her back. "It won't hurt, Glory. Now stand still."

Finally, Mag managed to get both saddle and blanket on the fidgeting pony, but not before she let Glory smell it and inspect it closely. Mag wiped her face on her shirttail. "Now, we're going for a little ride." But Glory had other ideas. She wanted Mag to crawl on, not to put her feet in the stirrups. The pony kept sidestepping. Finally, Mag broke a switch from a bush, fully intending to use it on Glory, as Warren had said. Glory apparently realized it and began to behave a little better.

"Now, that's better. You're really beautiful with a saddle on." She looked into Glory's face. The pony was crying. Mag was concerned. "I know it feels strange. I'm so sorry, but you'll get used to it. It isn't heavy or anything." Mag wiped the tears with her hand. When she was satisfied there were no more coming, she stroked the pony's neck and mounted.

She felt like a real cowgirl. "It's so comfortable. I'm going over now and show Ruth." Right away she decided against that. "I'll just wait until she comes over, and I'll let her use my saddle anytime she wants to." She felt good about her decision. She rode up to the porch and yelled for her parents to come see. She didn't know they had already been watching her through the window for some time.

They came out onto the porch, smiling. Mr. Henderson inspected the saddle. "Looks like you have it on her just like I told you, baby."

Mrs. Henderson remarked, "You look so pretty on your little saddled pony."

"I feel pretty, Mother. Oh, I'm so happy, I could fly over the house."

Mrs. Henderson laughed aloud. "Well, please don't. School starts soon, and I don't want any broken bones."

Mr. Henderson said, "Glory, you are really going to earn your keep at the plow and be a pleasure to Mag." Glory seemed to understand and bobbed her head up and down. They all laughed.

"I'm going to ride down the road."

Mag's parents nodded and watched her ride happily down the road, her tangled hair flying in the late summer breeze.

They looked at each other. "Henry, it's been a fine summer, hasn't it?"

Mr. Henderson pulled his pipe from his shirt pocket. "I'd say so. I guess you could say its been a Shetland summer all the way."

Mrs. Henderson laughed gently. Together, husband and wife went back into the house while Mag continued down the trail, singing a little cowboy song to Glory.

VISIT, WRITE or CALL your nearest ST. PAUL BOOK & MEDIA CENTER today for a wide selection of Catholic books, periodicals, cassettes, quality video cassettes for children and adults! Operated by the Daughters of St. Paul.

We are located in:

ALASKA
750 West 5th Ave., Anchorage, AK 99501 **907-272-8183.**
CALIFORNIA
3908 Sepulveda Blvd., Culver City, CA 90230 **213-397-8676; 213-398-6187.**
1570 Fifth Ave. (at Cedar Street), San Diego, CA 92101 **619-232-1442; 619-232-1443.**
46 Geary Street, San Francisco, CA 94108 **415-781-5180.**
FLORIDA
145 S.W. 107th Ave. Miami, FL 33174 **305-559-6715; 305-559-6716.**
HAWAII
1143 Bishop Street, Honolulu, HI 96813 **808-521-2731.**
ILLINOIS
172 North Michigan Ave., Chicago, IL 60601 **312-346-4228; 312-346-3240.**
LOUISIANA
423 Main Street, Baton Rouge, LA 70802 **504-343-4057.**
4403 Veterans Memorial Blvd., Metairie, LA 70006 **504-887-7631; 504-887-0113.**
MASSACHUSETTS
50 St. Paul's Ave., Jamaica Plain, Boston, MA 02130 **617-522-8911.**
Rte. 1, 450 Providence Hwy., Dedham, MA 02026 **617-326-5385.**
MISSOURI
9804 Watson Rd., St. Louis, MO 63126 **314-965-3512; 314-965-3571.**
NEW JERSEY
561 U.S. Route 1; No. C6, Wicks Plaza, Edison, NJ 08817 **201-572-1200; 201-572-1201.**
NEW YORK
150 East 52nd Street, New York, NY 10022 **212-754-1110.**
78 Fort Place, Staten Island, NY 10301 **718-447-5071; 718-447-5086.**
OHIO
2105 Ontario Street (at Prospect Ave.), Cleveland, OH 44115 **216-621-9427.**
PENNSYLVANIA
168 W. DeKalb Pike, King of Prussia, PA 19406 **215-337-1882; 215-337-2077.**
SOUTH CAROLINA
243 King Street, Charleston, SC 29401 **803-577-0175.**
TEXAS
114 Main Plaza, San Antonio, TX 78205 **512-224-8101.**
VIRGINIA
1025 King Street, Alexandria, VA 22314 **703-549-3806.**
CANADA
3022 Dufferin Street, Toronto, Ontario, Canada M6B 3T5 **416-781-9131.**